# THE POWER OF LOVE

a novel by
## KAMARAJU SUSILA

translated by
## UMA EACHEMPATI

This is a work of fiction. Any resemblance to actual events or locales or persons, living or dead, is merely coincidental, and names, characters, places, and incidents are either the products of the author's imagination or are used fictitiously.

For information, visit us at http://umaeachempati.homestead.com to learn more.

Cover by Kristina Blank Makansi, Treehouse Publishing Group

ISBN: 978-0-9914885-0-6

PREMA BALAM
For my parents
Kamaraju Susila


THE POWER OF LOVE
For my parents
Uma Eachempati

To Shakuntala &
Ashwath

with best wishes—
Uma Eec Lrmpee

# THE POWER OF LOVE

# Chapter One

It had become a habit in the life of Raja Rao to supervise the gardener each evening. He would go around the four corners of the garden and stand near each plant, checking that it had received enough manure and water.

One evening, Raja Rao was standing near the jasmine plant. He exclaimed to the gardener, "Mallaya, see how these jasmines are blossoming!"

"Oh, yes," said Mallaya with pride.

"Send the flowers inside to Amma garu."

"I do send them every day," replied Mallaya.

Raja Rao walked towards the house, removed the mud from his shoes at the veranda, and entered the hallway. Upon seeing the servant boy, Gangaram, at the entrance, he asked, "Is hot water ready for a bath?"

"Yes, sir," he replied with a blank face.

Raja Rao did not reply and went briskly inside.

Within fifteen minutes, he had bathed, put on the white *dhoti* and *lalchi* that the *dhobi* had brought, turned on the ceiling fan, and was sitting on the sofa, reaching out for the newspaper on the side table. The clerk, Subbiah, brought in some papers.

"What are those papers?" Raja Rao queried.

"We have to pay the taxes. These are related to that."

"Sit down." Raja Rao pointed to a chair beside him. Subbiah drew up a chair and sat down.

Subbiah's father had worked as manager for Raja Rao's father. As a child, Subbiah was very much a part of the household and part of the family. When Raja Rao took over the business, he enlisted Subbiah into the establishment.

"Did you bring the tax forms?" Raja Rao asked.

"Oh, yes." Subbiah handed him the forms and a pen.

Raja Rao signed at the specified areas and returned the papers.

"What is going on with our business?" Raja Rao said, taking a cigarette from his pocket and lighting it.

"Just like everything else, prices have gone up— even for clothes. So our business is booming. All three of our branches are packed with men and women at all times. I check on the accounts every day," Subbiah said.

"Do you remember the days of Father?"

"Why not? He started as a small business, ran a lorry service, and earned lakhs. His vigilance, his charity— he wouldn't refuse anyone who asked for help."

"Those days were different. It isn't the same nowadays."

"That's true."

"These days there is no happiness for the haves *or* for the have-nots." Raja Rao flicked the ash from the tip of the cigarette with his finger.

"You said it well. For people like us who live a

hand-to-mouth existence, not only Lord Brahma but the Trimurti have to descend to help us."

Raja Rao smiled at Subbiah's comment. "I am not going to rely on this business. I am educating my younger son to become a doctor, Subbiah. Just as a shine is important for gold, education is important for a man. What do you say?"

"Of course, sir!"

For a moment, Raja Rao fell into a reverie. "What is Amma garu doing?"

"She is supervising the making of the mango pickle."

"That means she will distribute the old pickle to all of you."

"Yes, sir. That has become the tradition."

"Telegram!" They heard a shout.

The telegram boy stood at the door. Subbiah received the telegram and handed it to Raja Rao. Subbiah signed the receipt, dispatched the delivery boy, and approached Raja Rao, who opened the envelope in a hurry.

"Ayyo! Subbiah!" Raja Rao was agitated upon reading the contents.

"What happened, sir?" Subbiah asked, showing concern.

Without replying to him, Raja Rao rushed into the kitchen, shouting, "Lalita!" with a racing heart.

"Lalita! Where are you?" he shouted again.

"What? What happened?" Lalita came to him.

"He's gone! Brother-in-law! He's gone." Raja Rao slumped into a chair.

"Which brother-in-law?" Lalita questioned.

"What do you mean, which brother-in-law?

Purnamma's husband," Raja Rao growled, grief-stricken.

"*Hayyo!* What horror is this? When did he pass away?"

"The day before yesterday. They sent an urgent telegram the very same night, but we just got it today!"

"Wonder what illness?"

"It was not an illness. It was an accident," he said curtly.

"Subbiah!" Raja Rao shouted.

Subbiah, standing nearby, approached, terrified. "Yes, sir."

"I have to go to Madras on tonight's train. Get the car out. You must also come with me to the station."

"All the formalities will be over by now. What will you do by going in such a hurry? For the tenth day—" Lalita drawled.

Even before she could finish the sentence, Raja Rao cut her off. "Are you out of your mind? She is my only sister, and she is younger than me. When she is crying at the loss of her husband, you are suggesting to me to wait ten days! Go and pack my bags!" Raja Rao screamed.

As there was nothing else to say or do, Lalita packed the box and brought it out in half an hour.

The bond between Raja Rao's family and Subbiah was unimaginable. Subbiah was relied upon for errands in the house as well as anything concerning the business. Everything went through him. But he did not intrude in family matters or give his opinion. Still, being a well-wisher of the family, he shared Raja Rao's heartache at the loss of Purnamma's husband. He had tears in his eyes. Wiping them, Subbiah picked up the bags and announced that the car was ready.

"All right, let's go." Raja Rao looked towards his wife. "Lalita, I need one thousand rupees." Being a careful man, Raja Rao always kept about two thousand rupees in the house. One could never tell when the necessity would arise.

"What will possibly cost one thousand rupees? Maybe he will buy a white saree. There is no need for a blouse piece even," Lalita muttered, giving her husband the thousand rupees, which he placed in his purse.

"I am bringing Purnamma and Malati along with me," he announced as he walked out the door.

Lalita followed him to the car.

"*Emandi*, if you don't mind, listen to what I have to say. Women know more about these matters than men do. Do you really think your sister will accompany you now?"

"If she does not, I will coax and cajole her until she does."

"You are leaving without having your dinner?"

"I will eat somewhere." He was abrupt.

"It is getting late," shouted Subbiah.

After the luggage was loaded, Raja Rao got into the car. The car went out the gate. Lalita, absorbed in her own thoughts, sat down with a thud on a cane chair in the veranda.

"Ayyagaru left without eating. Should I serve you?" the cook asked, coming into the veranda. Lalita came out of her trance.

"Yes, I am coming. Let's go." She rose from the chair.

She lay in bed after dinner with her thoughts

rushing in waves.

*It is better to be frank at the outset, than at the end. If Purnamma and Malati come here, there are sure to be misunderstandings. Better to throw some money at them and have them stay in their own dwelling. That would be best for everyone. Poor man, Purnamma's father-in-law! Has anyone thought of what is going on with the old man? In his old age, he is crying for a dead son. Everyone is being selfish and taking care of his or her own comfort and happiness.*

Lalita was bitter and harsh.

# Chapter Two

As soon as they reached the station, Subbiah ran in and bought one ticket to Madras for Raja Rao and a platform ticket for himself. He settled the box under the berth, spread the bedding over it, and waited on the platform with Raja Rao.

"It is time; please get inside," Subbiah said.

Raja Rao got onto the train. "You can go home. It is already late—your family will be waiting for you."

"It is all right. Somehow we made it to the train."

One man was shouting, "Bananas! Bananas!"

"Cashews!" shouted another. A young man pushing a cart with biscuits and other eatables was followed by another who had books and magazines. Some coolies were taking away their empty luggage carts.

"The Madras Mail will be leaving from Platform Number One," said the announcer on the public system in Telugu, English, and Hindi.

"I will return on the thirteenth day. Bring the car to the station," Raja Rao instructed.

"All right." Subbiah reinforced his words by rotating his head.

The hustle on the platform subsided. The guard waved his green flag. The long train filled with hundreds of passengers lurched forward and puffed away, heaving like a pregnant woman at term, then gradually picked up speed. Raja Rao looked out the window. The scenes were competing with the train, running along with it. But Raja Rao's mind was rummaging the past. He did not notice the scenery.

# Chapter Three

Rajashekhar Rao and Annapurna were parents of Padmanabham, who named his own children after them in gratitude. The first child was a boy, and then four years later, a girl was born. In daily parlance, they became Raja Rao and Purnamma.

Padmanabham rented some lorries, and with this service earned his fortune. From the profits, he started Padmanabha Silk House, which soon expanded into three branches. He desired to give his son a good university education, but Raja Rao obtained a BA degree with great difficulty. Padmanabham accepted the fact that the Goddess of Learning, Saraswati, had not favored his son.

Raja Rao's mother, Kamakshamma, carried out her household duties diligently. Friends and relatives were welcome at her home at all times. Being devout, she performed *Tulsi Puja* every day. She also invited the neighborhood women to come for many pujas and chants. She would have gatherings where the *Gita* and *Ramayana* were read.

Purnamma quit school at the age of fourteen to stay

home and learn household duties. When she turned eighteen, her father arranged a marriage to an "only son." The wedding was celebrated with great pomp and splendor, as was befitting his social status.

On the day of the wedding, Purnamma had the traditional *Mangala Snana* and decked herself in a Benares silk saree. Her feet were decorated with turmeric and red dye. The traditional red dot of marriage adorned her forehead, and the black dot to ward off evil eyes decorated her cheek. With jasmine flowers wound around her long braid, Purnamma looked divine. However, there was no trace of happiness either on the face of the bride or of her mother. But Raja Rao hoped this was natural for the mother of the bride.

The bride was seated next to the groom in the decorated tent. To the beat of the traditional drums and pipes, Rama Rao tied the *mangalasutra* round her neck. Colored rice, showering blessings, fell on them from all corners of the tent. Following the sacred promises with the "seven steps," they exchanged the pouring of colored rice to signify prosperity and happiness. They bowed and took the blessings of all the elders. Purnamma cleared her saree of the rice and approached her mother, then drooped over her shoulder and sobbed. Kamakshamma, wiping her own tears, held her daughter to her bosom before she let her go out of her parental home. This sight tugged at Raja Rao's heart.

To live the rest of her life with another human being—the man who tied the three knots round her neck—seemed a formidable task at this young age. These young women must have patience, forbearance, strength, and a capacity for compromise in order to live together in harmony with a spouse. He was appalled. His father had furthered his education, but denied the sister who was meritorious in class.

Now, she was leaving her maternal home.

Raja Rao was wistful.

At the time of the wedding, Purnamma's husband, Rama Rao, was a law student in Madras. Padmanabhan opined that Purnamma could join her husband after his graduation, but Rama Rao firmly expressed his right. He had not gotten married to leave his wife behind with her parents. His mother had died, and there was no woman to run the household. So Purnamma, traveling with her father, uncle, and husband, left for Madras. But Purnamma was unhappy there. The house consisted of two rooms separated by an open space. Of the two rooms, one was a kitchen, which did not have a proper window. It was dark, so she kept the light on all day.

In order to reach the college on time, Rama Rao left home at nine in the morning to catch the bus. Purnamma woke at five in the morning to get his food ready. She struggled with these demands.

# Chapter Four

Raja Rao did not notice the number of stations the train had passed. He was thinking of his sister with sadness. Fifteen years ago, Purnamma, pregnant with Malati, had to be brought to the maternal home as was the custom. Padmanabham wrote to her father-in-law and husband individually. They replied that Purna would stay in Madras for the childbirth as there were many good doctors and hospitals in the city. Kamakshamma wished to go to Madras to help her daughter, but the offer was rejected as unnecessary.

A few months later, Kamakshamma got sick, and the doctors gave up hope. She wished to see her daughter one last time. A telegram was sent informing Purna of the news of Kamakshamma's terminal illness and her desire to see her daughter, asking to please send Purnamma home. Since the expenses were not paid for, the husband did not send her. In the end, Kamakshamma passed on without seeing her daughter. Purnamma agonized, as she could not see her mother one last time. Four years later, when Padmanabham got sick, Raja Rao sent a telegram to his sister and sent the fare for her travel. Purnamma arrived with her daughter, Malati. Four days later, Padmanabham died, and Purnamma left after fifteen days. Again today, Purnamma lamented the sudden loss of her husband. Raja Rao's heart melted thinking of his sister.

Rama Rao, Purnamma's husband, entered law college but failed the exams after many years. After three to four attempts, he dropped the idea of obtaining a law degree. His father decided that Purnamma's bad luck caused his son's failure. He declared that it is the wife's destiny that makes her husband a success. Raja Rao recollected every unpleasant event that occurred in the past. He recalled the words his mother spoke the day before she closed her eyes: "Dear Raja, you are the heir to all this property. This is my only request from you. Your sister has no happiness in her husband's house. I do not know what is in store for her in the future. We thought her husband would be a successful lawyer, but he has not even passed the exam and has quit. We can give her any amount of gold, but some day you will have to take over her care." She clutched his hand.

"Amma, do not worry about Purna. I will do whatever is possible for her," Raja Rao encouraged his mother in her last moments.

"Since you have reassured me, I will not worry about her," said his mother. She died the next day.

All the unpleasantness, scene after scene, rolled through his head like a reel of a movie. The train reached Central Station in Madras. Raja Rao picked up his box and bedding and went to Tiruvallicane in a taxi, to his sister's house. The door was ajar. He pushed it open and entered. He found his sister sitting on the floor, leaning against the wall. She looked beaten and ten years older, a face smeared with misery. Unable to contain her sorrow, Purna burst into tears on seeing her brother. He sat near her patting her head, consoling her. Malati, her daughter, entered the room from the kitchen.

"Who has come?" asked Rama Rao's father from inside.

"It is Uncle," replied Malati.

"Who is it? Raja Rao?" The old man accosted him walking towards him. "When did you come?"

"Just now. The train was four and half hours late."

"See what destiny has decided. I am an old man, and she takes him," he said with a sigh.

"Who is the creator of one's destiny? It is not in our hands. It will be as Brahma has written," said Raja Rao.

"It is not Brahma's writing. Actually, Rama Rao was very careless. I have been warning him to be careful from the time he bought the scooter, but he does not take anyone's advice," said the old man, sick at heart.

"When did the accident happen?" asked Raja Rao.

"Monday morning," said Purnamma. "Just like any day, he said that he needed to go out on an errand. As he found it difficult to ride the bus, I asked him to buy a scooter. It is not even three months since he bought it."

"When did you hear about the accident?" asked Raja Rao.

"It probably happened at ten o'clock in the morning. The police looked at the address in his diary, and by noon, they were home to inform us. They left the body in the hospital morgue. I went with the police for identification. But what is there? The very much smashed body was difficult to identify. They wanted a postmortem. Night fell when all these were done, so we went to the cremation ground straight from the hospital. Why should we bring him home? What will anyone see? Nothing to be shown—" and he paused. After a while, he composed himself. "Actually, he is a careless fellow. Anger. Ego. High on stubbornness and low on caution."

"Why should we say that about the dead?" Purnamma interrupted.

"I am not just saying it; I just want to tell your brother what kind of a man he was."

Malati handed over the glass of coffee to Raja Rao.

"You brought coffee! Maybe he wants to have a bath and have lunch," said the old man.

"It's all right," said Raja Rao and drank the coffee.

The old man went in and sat in the folding easy chair.

"I thought that you would be coming yesterday," said Purnamma.

"I left as soon as I received the telegram."

"Only those close to Father-in-law were sent telegrams. The rest were sent postcards."

Stillness was in the air.

"Malati is the only one left to do the housework and the errands outside. She is taking care of everything," said Purnamma

Malati sat on the floor leaning against the opposite wall.

"Did you check if there is water in the bathroom?" asked Purnamma looking towards Malati.

"Yes, there is; I just collected the water."

"I will have a bath," Raja Rao said and went to the bathroom. Malati followed him.

"Be careful, Uncle, it is a little slippery."

All right, child." Raja Rao looked at Malati, bright and divine like the Goddess Lakshmi. By the time he finished his bath, Malati placed the wooden seat to sit on and a silver plate in front of it. Raja Rao wiped his face with a towel and sat down to eat. Malati talked her heart out while serving him.

"Mother got the spices ready for the annual making of the mango pickle and wanted to buy the green mangoes. In the meantime, all this commotion happened," said Malati woefully.

Raja Rao ate a few morsels and joined Purnamma. Rama Rao's passing did not affect his father, Purna, or Malati as much as Raja Rao expected. They were not as weak as he thought they would be. Days went by. All the rituals were followed by the old man without much fuss. According to tradition, on the thirteenth day, the *rangoli* was drawn at the front entrance and sweet *payas* was made. After lunch, Raja Rao approached Purna about travel plans.

"I plan to leave today and want to take you and Malati along with me. What do you say?"

"What can I say? I don't think this is a good time for me to accompany you."

Why won't it be good? So when do you think you can come?"

Malati joined in. "Uncle, I have finished school this year. All my classmates are moving on to college. You have to consider my studies, also, don't you think?"

"Higher studies are not that simple. That is not for us. You can join some typing classes," said Purna.

"Whatever you want to do, you have to apply now, as the classes will start soon after the summer holidays," said Raja Rao.

"So, what do you think?" asked Purna.

"I want both of you to come with me," Raja Rao said, sounding inflexible.

"What will Father-in-law say?"

"Ask him."

Purna went to her father-in-law hesitatingly.

"Brother wants to take me to Visakhapatnam with him," Purna mumbled.

"If he wants to take you, you can go," he said in a bland tone.

Purna, shaken, crept out of the room.

"I don't think Father-in-law will like us to leave now; we will come later," Purna reported to Raja Rao.

"Why won't he like it? You should tell him decidedly that it is for Malati's education."

"How can I tell him firmly?"

"I will tell him," Raja Rao said and went into the old man's room.

"Whatever needs to be done here has been concluded today. Is it not? So grant me permission to leave," he said politely.

"What is it? I hear that your sister and Malati are also going with you."

"It will be good if they come. We have to consider Malati's higher education."

"What about her studies? She is a girl. To what purpose, studies?"

"What, Grandpa! Are my studies a minor matter? I am going with Uncle, even if mother does not come," Malati announced.

"After the decision has been made by all of you, there is no need to ask me," said the old man harshly.

"If Malati is definitely accompanying me, what will Purna do here all by herself?"

"All right, go," said the old man, chewing his words.

Malati, excited about the decision, pulled out a box and threw in all her old clothes, some new clothes, her mother's clothes, and other things they would need—all in a jiffy.

After her husband's loss, Purna did not think that she belonged here anymore. In all these years, never had a kind word been uttered by her father-in-law. Did he at least speak to his son, who was maybe a vagabond, even once with affection? It was due to the woman's inefficiency that he had become a good-for-nothing. It was all her fault. When his son failed in the exams, he considered it his bad luck. The wife's bad luck took his son's life. But who can deny it?

Taunted by these thoughts Purna decided to leave for Visakhapatnam with her brother. She went into the kitchen to organize and clean the kitchen before she left. Raja Rao called out to Purna as he entered the kitchen.

"What did you say?" Purna turned around.

"Do you have all your jewels?" he asked timidly.

Purna's face changed colors.

"I have some, not all," she replied falteringly.

"What do you mean, not all? Where have they gone?"

"We sold it for necessities."

'What was the necessity that you had to sell your gold?"

"What was the cause—? My husband failed his

law exams four times. Later he set up a business with one of his friends, and for that he needed thousands and thousands for the security. The best friend said that the profits were his, and the losses were ours. My husband realized that this man was no good. They quarreled. The so-called friend said he had evidence and threatened to report it to the police and have my husband arrested. There was a tremendous loss in the business. After that, he started a radio repair shop. One night the shop was burglarized, and all the radios were stolen. The customers whose radios were there for repair—will they keep quiet? They sued, and all of them had to be compensated. For all this, how could you manage without selling the gold?" she said dejected.

"Whatever has happened has happened. Bring whatever you have left."

After straightening out the kitchen, Purna went to her father-in-law's room.

"Tonight we are leaving with my brother," she said faintly.

"Yes I know; your brother told me. This old man can join any river. What do you care?"

Purna was mute.

"Here, these are all Rama Rao's insurance policies. There seems to be some money in the bank. You take care of these after you reach Vizag. I cannot give you any more than this."

Purna accepted them all and carefully packed them in her box. She was ready for the journey. Raja Rao called for a taxi to take them to the station. Purna and Malati bowed at the old man's feet.

"I'll come," said Raja Rao and sat in the passenger

seat. Purna and Malati sat at the back. The old man watched the luggage being loaded in the dickey and the taxi drive away.

"Go to Central Station via the beach," Raja Rao instructed the driver.

With the cool breeze on her face, Malati looked at the ocean, excited to see the rolling waves and the small boats on the water.

"Amma, did you see the small boats?"

"Yes, I see them," said her mother, sounding relieved.

"Uncle, there is an ocean and beach even in Vizag, isn't there?"

"Yes, dear," Raja Rao said, his mind far away.

Malati felt as if released from prison. She eagerly awaited a new place, a new town, and new experiences.

The taxi arrived at Central Station. Malati did not remember riding a train. It was all a dream. The luggage was loaded on the trolley; the coolie directed them to the train to Vizag. The three followed him. He kept the luggage in the railway compartment and collected his money. Purna counted the pieces of luggage, and she made herself comfortable. Malati, seated at the window, looked onto the platform. The noisy platform was filled with swiftly walking men and women, young and old, wearing a variety of clothing, searching for their reservations. Some coolies were waiting for their money. Some collected theirs and were soliciting the next job. The coolies who were pushing the trollies laden with luggage were saying, "*Voram voram*," in Tamil, asking people to move aside, weaving their way through the crowd.

A loud announcement by a masculine voice about the arrival and departure of trains, with details of the platform numbers, was heard. Malati looked at the world like a newborn opening her eyes for the first time to the light. Purna sat quietly next to her.

"Has all the luggage arrived?" said Raja Rao peering through the window.

"Yes, it has," Purna replied.

"I will go to the restaurant and check it out," said Raja Rao. He returned in fifteen minutes.

"They ran out of the *sambhar* rice, so he gave me some *upma*. I will get some fruit, and we can manage for tonight," Raja Rao said.

"Why do we need all this?" said Purna, accepting the packets.

"I will drink a soda. Do any of you need any colors?"

"I don't need colors or cola. You can get your soda," said Purna.

"Malati, dear, do you want me to get you anything?"

"No, I don't need anything," said Malati.

"You are back so soon," said Purna a short time later. "Didn't you get a soda?"

"I could not find any soda place," said Raja Rao. "Never mind." He had bought the latest edition of *The Hindu*. Soon the bustle subsided, and the train started moving. Raja Rao was reading the paper, Malati looked out the window in awe, and Purna was in a daze.

# Chapter Five

Lalita, fuming that her husband was bringing his sister and niece, made sleeping arrangements by taking out beds and mattresses for them. In the meantime, Subbiah stood near the doorstep saying, "Amma garu!"

"What is it, Subbiah?" Lalita stepped outside.

"Ayya is coming in today's mail. He wanted the car to be brought to the station. Should I take it?" he asked in a subdued voice.

"Subbiah, have you ever seen anything stranger than this?"

"What, Amma?" He sounded nervous.

"When your husband dies, they say you should not go anywhere for one year. Why does that Purna have to come here now?"

Subbiah understood the thought behind the words. He recollected Raja Rao mentioning that he would bring his sister and niece, even if he had to beg them.

"Ayya is a very soft-hearted man, Amma," he said softly.

"Men do not know these matters, and they will not listen. She does not have to come here to mourn," she said sharply.

After a moment's silence, Subbiah repeated, "Shall I take the car?"

"Yes, take it. Cannot escape this," she snapped.

Subbiah was about to leave.

"Subbiah!" He halted. "Take the old car, not the new one. The battery is low for the old car. It needs a run." Lalita looked at him sternly for a moment "All right. What can one do? Go."

Subbiah left quietly, amused.

*Battery is down. Life itself is going down frightfully. My house, my home, my reign,* Lalita thought.

All these years, whatever Lalita played and whatever she sang was catered to. In that house, her every wish was a command. She ruled single-handedly. Her husband never contradicted her. Now, another woman was coming into the house, HIS sister! She would be treated with affection and respect. Lalita would have to share everything from now on, even though her husband respected her and gave her plenty of attention.

Purna was not coming today and leaving tomorrow. She would be here permanently. Raja Rao promised his dying mother that he would take care of her, and now he was fulfilling that promise. So hereafter it would be a "party" for this old woman. Lalita was perturbed. She heard the sound of a car stopping at the front gate and went to the veranda. Purna alighted from the car. She made her formal entry into the house. Yes, she did enter with the traditional right foot first for her homecoming. This revolted Lalita. She went up to Purna, put her arm around her, and took her inside. On seeing her sister-in-law, tears welled up in Purna's eyes.

"Sister-in-law! Today I am forced to return to this house, grieving," Purna wailed, wiping her tears.

"No, No, this is no stranger's house," consoled Lalita.

"Because this is not a stranger's house, I agreed to come when Brother asked me to."

Malati stood in silence. She donned the beauty and innocence of her age, with attractive eyes, golden skin, and long braided hair. Subbiah unloaded the car and supervised the carrying of the luggage into the house. Malati and Raja Rao also entered the house.

"Is Bhaskar here?" Raja Rao inquired about his son.

"He's gone to college and said that he would be back early since all of you were arriving," said Lalita.

Who? Bhaskar?" Purna was sitting on the sofa in the hallway. "Bhaskar is a medical student, isn't he?" asked Purna.

"Yes. This is his last year."

"I last saw him at Father's funeral."

"Yes, you did not come back after that," said Lalita. The cook brought the coffee tray and set it on the table. Lalita gave one glass to Purna. Malati picked up a glass and said, "How about you, Auntie?"

"I will have it; you have yours."

Some minutes passed in silence.

"These accidents: how many families get crushed with these accidents? When one leaves the house, there is no knowing until you return," said Lalita.

"It is all our bad luck," said Purna, laying the empty glass on the table.

"Ayya is asking for you," said Subbiah, and Lalita went inside.

Malati looked around the four corners of the house

with awe. How beautiful the house was! There were
two photos on the wall with garlands around them.
She guessed that they would be her dead grandparents.
The photo of a young man in a silver frame placed on
the table attracted Malati's attention.

"Amma, is this Bhaskar's photo?" Her mother
nodded to mean, "Yes." Malati got up and studied
the photo keenly. She felt as if the eyes were looking
deeply into hers. She pondered for a moment.

"Handsome guy," she said out loud without
meaning to.

"Yes, he is a handsome boy. I saw him a long time
ago when he was just a kid," said Purna.

Malati looked around, appreciative of the décor.
The house sparkled. There were pots in a row on the
veranda, with colorful flowers in bloom.

The cook cleared the coffee glasses.

"Look here, in which room have you placed our
luggage?" Purna asked Gangaram.

"There, in the room opposite," he said, pointing to
the room.

"All right." Purna went into the room. Malati
stopped at the photo for a couple more minutes and
then joined her mother.

# Chapter Six

Lunch being over, everyone was asleep in the afternoon. After the strain of the journey and the ritualistic baths of the funeral, Purna fell into a deep slumber with the cool breeze from the ceiling fan. Malati, bored, wandered around. Bhaskar returned from college at three o'clock in the afternoon. He went to his room, freshened up, and sat at the dining table for his lunch. Malati passed through the dining room on her way to the kitchen and returned with a water glass in hand.

"Hullo," said Bhaskar. Malati stopped a second and left the room. Bhaskar smiled. He finished his meal and went out on his scooter. Malati followed his movements in silence.

That evening, Raja Rao supervised the planting of new shrubs by the gardener, Mallaya. The servant boy brought some lawn chairs into the garden for Purna and Malati to sit on. Bhaskar returned home and, on seeing them on the front lawn, pulled up a chair and sat down next to his aunt.

"When I came home from college in the afternoon,

you were sleeping," he said.

"Yes, son, I don't know. I went into a very deep sleep such that I was unaware of anything."

"I saw Malati," he said, looking in her direction. Malati looked down at the ground.

"What is Malati doing now?" Bhaskar asked his aunt.

"Ask her yourself."

Bhaskar looked at Malati questioningly.

"I finished my school final."

"What are you going to do now?"

"Uncle said he would look into it."

"You have to apply soon for whatever it is. It is already late."

"She will learn some typing. I don't want to further her studies," said Purna.

Raja Rao joined them.

"You seem to have planted a lot of new plants," said Purna to her brother.

"Must have some hobby," he said, smiling.

"If you finish your bath, we can have dinner," yelled Lalita from the veranda.

"Let's also go," said Purna, rising.

Everyone went back inside the house. After ten minutes, Raja Rao sat at the dining table where everyone was already seated. The maid, Chukkamma, stood near the door of the kitchen. The cook brought some steaming, aromatic potato and onion curry.

"You cooked onions?" said Malati softly.

"Don't you like onions?" asked Raja Rao.

"It does not matter for one meal," interjected Purna.

"These things should have been checked before cooking," Raja Rao said.

Lalita was irritated. Malati bent her head in regret, and Purna was uncomfortable.

"Ramayya, hereafter, do not even get the smell of onions into the house," said Lalita to the cook.

"Young master likes onions in all his food," said the cook casually.

"If young master likes it, this young lady does not," said Lalita sharply.

"It is all right," said Malati, stuttering.

"I also don't like onions," said Raja Rao, bemused.

"After all these years, I know today that you do not like onions," Lalita said with venom.

Raja Rao gave a low laugh.

"I will cook without onions for the young lady. That is no problem," Ramayya announced as a reply to all.

"No one has the sense that Ramayya has," said Raja Rao.

Silence ate the rest of the meal.

# Chapter Seven

A week went by without any confrontations. Lalita had a staff of servants for the various household chores, and there was no opportunity for Purna to help and get involved. She stayed in her own room. Malati, not knowing what to do in the new place, wandered around the garden. Bhaskar came home early one day. He drove the car when he did not take the scooter. On seeing Malati in the garden, he walked up to her and noticed she was a little flustered at his approach.

"Do you like flowers and flowering plants?" he asked.

"Why? Don't you like them?"

"All beautiful things attract me, *Poolu, Maalu*," he said mischievously.

Malati felt shy.

Having heard the sound of the car and wondering why Bhaskar did not come in, Lalita came out. She cringed on seeing Malati and Bhaskar together.

"Bhaskar!" she called with an unkind voice.

"Coming!" Bhaskar went in.

"It is a new place, and she is feeling embarrassed.

Why do you go near her?" Lalita warned.

"What new place?"

Both went into the house.

# Chapter Eight

Days were flying by. Lalita would grumble now and again. She herself did not seem to know why unhappiness befriended her. THEY were all one. She felt isolated.

One day, Bhaskar was home as usual at three in the afternoon and peeped into Malati's room and found her sewing.

"You did not go to the garden today?"

"She is bored. Why don't you bring her some Telugu books to read?" her mother replied.

"What, Malati? Are you bored?"

Malati shook her head to say, "No," without raising it.

"All right, I will have my lunch and we can play chess," he said.

"I don't know how to play."

"I can teach you," he said and skipped out of the room.

In half an hour, he returned with the board and pieces.

"Let us go to the veranda. There is a cool breeze,

too."

Malati followed him. He set up the pieces on the board.

"Do you know the names of all these?" he asked.

"Yes, I do."

"Oh! So you just don't know how to play." He smiled.

She nodded to mean, "Yes."

"After two games, you will know how to play."

He explained the game to her, and she picked up the rules quickly. Laughs and giggles were heard, but Malati was coy. Lalita came to the veranda and saw them. The indefinable hurt increased by the minute. She could not contain herself.

"Bhaskar! This year is your final exams. If you keep playing around, singing and dancing, wasting your time, you are going to regret it later," she warned. As expected, they paid no attention and continued to play chess every day in the veranda.

As days went by Malati, grew familiar and was not as shy anymore. She would argue with Bhaskar, her voice and laughter increasing in pitch. He lost to her deliberately and, each time she won, would hold her hand, shake it vigorously, and say, "Congratulations."

One day while playing, she said, "*Bava*" (the common name for a male kissing cousin). His face lit up, and he responded tenderly: "Malati." At that sacred moment, the friendship brewing between them received a stamp of love.

The next day, Malati and Bhaskar went to the veranda and were again with the chess board in front of them. They were laughing and looking at each other without reason. Lalita watched them from a distance.

*If this friendship between them turns into love, Bhaskar might refuse to marry anyone else,* she thought. Her husband was known to do exactly as he wanted. He called Malati, "The Unblemished One" (Chakkati Chukka), "Star of all Gems" (Ratnalarasi), and if he made Malati the daughter-in-law of the house, Lalita would have no status or respect in her own house. There would be a transfer of power in the house, just as it happened in Delhi on August 15, 1947, when India gained independence from the British.

These thoughts consumed her. The head got heavy with anxiety; her face did not grow pink like the vegetable yam, but red as a ripe tomato. Fuming with anger and intolerance, Lalita roared, "Malati!" in a demoniac frenzy.

Bhaskar realized that his mother was having a "panic attack" and went and held her. Malati was immobilized like a charmed snake. Purna, Raja Rao, and all the servants rushed out. Raja Rao and Bhaskar supported Lalita on either side and took her in and lay her down on the bed.

What happened and why it happened—neither the final-year medical student nor the man with forty-five birthdays could understand. Purna understood Lalita's roar, "MALATI!" Subbiah suspected the meaning nested in that.

Lalita lay in bed, frustrated, whining. *They have laid me down here. They have won by hurting me. The arrival of Purna and Malati is for the worst, not the best.*

This thought pounded in her head like the shattering of a clay pot. She had told her husband on the day of their arrival that it is better to be up front and clarify things in the beginning. What she realized, her husband did not, no matter how much she yelled at him. What is the use of yelling in a house where your word is not heard and you receive no respect? He promised his mother; today he was fulfilling that promise to the fullest. He would not break his word. Another incarnation of Lord Rama, "Oh God," she exclaimed.

Fifteen days after the loss of her husband, as if the world came to an end without looking for the appropriate lunar day, she arrived. If she was firm about coming here later, what could this brother have done? Just for the asking, Purna packed up and landed here without any shame or modesty. Having no thoughts about the welfare of the old father-in-law, and leaving the funeral rites unfinished, she happily left everything and arrived here. The old man is stumbling along, as he cannot even see well.

No one told her, but Lalita presumed that being an old man he must be blind and stumbling in his path. She rolled in bed, with these words keeping her awake. She cursed circumstances and was deep in thought. The disturbed mind prevented her from sleep for a long time. Gradually, she fell into a deep slumber.

# Chapter Nine

Purna went to Lalita's room early in the morning and called out, "Sister-in-law, how are you? Did you sleep well?"

'Why? I am fine. Looks like all of you were chatting in the hall for a long time," Lalita replied.

"Yes, Brother was very worried, and he could not sleep, so we all sat up with him and chatted." Purna expressed her concerns.

"What is there to chat about?" Lalita said, disgusted.

"Oh, some childhood memories—shall I bring you some coffee? If you brush your teeth, I will bring the coffee."

"Yes, I have finished brushing my teeth. Why should you bring the coffee? What happened to that Chukkamma?"

Purna returned in five minutes with the coffee.

"Brother said that if you rest all day today, you will feel better by evening." Purna handed the glass of coffee. Lalita reached out for the glass with the thought, *If I am at permanent rest, you would take control of the house and the running of it and be very happy.*

Purna took the empty glass and left the room.

"Lalita, how are you, dear? Have you had your coffee?" said Raja Rao entering the room.

"How am I? I have no disease. I am fine," she replied grumpily.

"Who said you have a disease? We were all worried last night and were going to call the doctor this morning."

"There is no need for any doctors," she mumbled.

"Yes, if you rest all day, you should be fine by evening. Don't worry about the household chores; Purna can take care of it."

"You brought her here as she was grieving; why do you burden her with the chores?" Lalita was being very considerate.

"She will take care of things until you feel better. I will tell Purna before I leave."

"You are not supposed to ask, 'Where are you going,' but where are you headed to?"

"I am going to the bazaar. Do you need anything?"

"I don't need anything. Come back soon."

"As you say," he said and left the room.

"Look here!" she yelled after him.

"What is it?" He turned around.

"I am not able to stay alone in this room. Please ask Malati to keep me company."

"Sure. That girl has spunk. If she could be our daughter-in-law, you wouldn't have to get down from the bed," he said, content.

Lalita sat up with a start. "You are telling me that I don't have to get out of bed. Don't make any such promise. You mean to say I am going to be sick for a long time?"

"Lalita! Anything I say, you twist it around. I am leaving."

"Look, send Malati."

"All right."

"Auntie, did you want me to come?" said Malati the next minute.

Lalita stared at Malati. The girl was pretty, and that was the reason for all problems to raise their heads.

"What were you doing?" she asked rudely.

"Nothing," Malati replied casually.

"Whatever book that you were reading out there, bring it here and read it. I am not able to stay alone."

"Sure, Auntie. I will have a bath and come back," she said and disappeared. Malati returned a half hour later, book in hand, and pulled a chair close to Lalita's bed and sat down.

Lalita closed her eyes. Malati was immersed in her book.

Bhaskar entered the room.

"How are you, Mother?" he asked.

"I am fine, but haven't you gone to college yet?"

"Today I am going a little bit late," he said and tapped Malati on the head as he exited. Malati suppressed a giggle. Lalita felt as if caterpillars were crawling all over her. This is their behavior in front of me! She disapproved of it and looked at Malati with hate.

That evening when Bhaskar returned from college, Malati was still in Lalita's room. He stood at the door and signaled to Malati to come out, and she stepped out.

"Come, let's play chess," he said.

"Aunt is unable to stay alone."

"Your mother can keep her company," Bhaskar said and went into Purna's room. "Aunt, would you stay a while with my mother?"

"Sure," said Purna, and she went to Lalita's room. Lalita had her eyes closed. Purna sat in the chair quietly. A few minutes later, Lalita opened her eyes and saw Purna.

"When did you come? Where is Malati?"

"I have been here a while. Bhaskar and Malati are playing chess in the veranda."

Lalita drew a long sigh.

"Purna, the children are immersed in the game of chess; they are in it always. This is his final year in college, and if he keeps wasting his time this way, the exams will climb the tree," she heaved.

Purna was jolted. She wanted to shake Malati as well.

# Chapter Ten

Purna was in turmoil about her broken life. Today she stood in the shade of her brother. What about the future? Everything was confusing. Even though Brother respected her, she had no status here. Going back to a parent's house was shameful for a married woman. But how can one survive going back to a brother *and* sister-in-law? This was not for one day.

*I do not know how long this life will last,* she thought. *I must think of Malati's future. The husband dying suddenly, my brother bringing me here to Vizag, the decision to accompany him: they all happened within moments. I made imprudent decisions without thinking through the consequences. Did I make a mistake by coming here?* Scared, she fell asleep.

Purna woke up at five as the sun shone through the window; she heard the sounds of the streets and the dog barking next door. She saw Malati sleeping on the cot next to hers, her long braid dangling from the bed. She opened her eyes just for one long look at Malati, turned over, and went to sleep. In the meantime, the maid, Chukamma, stood near the doorstep.

"Amma garu wanted me to tell you that the maid who is to wash dishes has called in sick today," she announced like the news on All India Radio.

Purna understood the message and quickly brushed her teeth and went towards the pump where the dirty dishes were placed. The cook added a few more dishes. Purna washed them.

"Is coffee ready?" said Raja Rao as he entered the kitchen. "What, Purna, you here?" he said, surprised on seeing Purna at the pump.

"Chukamma told me the maid did not come," Purna said in a long drawl.

"If the maid does not come, there are others. Come on, get up," he said in anger.

With the coffee glass given to him by the cook in one hand, and the morning's paper in the other, Raja Rao went to Lalita's room from the kitchen. Lalita stood in front of him.

"The maid did not come, and so Purna is washing the dishes," he said as if lodging a complaint.

"What, the maid did not come? If we have a couple of extra guests, they happily quit work," Lalita said, as if fed up with the situation.

"Pay them some extra. Why should Purna wash dishes?"

Lalita went to the backyard.

"*Hayyo!* What sin is this? Purna! Enough of washing dishes. Wash your hands and get up."

"I am almost done, only two more dishes. I will finish them," said Purna.

"All these! So many dishes! You finished them in minutes! You have a talent for working. But your brother thinks that I have put you to work."

"Nothing wrong in doing our household chores," said Purna.

"When there are a houseful of people, why do you have to wash the dishes, dear?" Raja Rao asked Purna.

"Purna is used to menial work," Lalita butted in.

"Shut up," Raja Rao said.

Lalita was taken aback. Purna at the pump was shaken.

*Not minding the presence of Chukamma and the cook, for him to insult me like that*—tears welled up in Lalita's eyes. *It has not even been a month, and the situation has taken a grave turn. Wonder what else is in store, thought Lalita.*

Purna finished the dishes, wiped her hands with the corner of her saree, and entered the room.

"Have you had your coffee?" asked Raja Rao.

"I have come here only to eat and drink," replied Purna, hurt.

"Oh, sister! From today, please do not come out of your room. If you walk, your feet—and if you work, your hands—will get worn out. So thinks your dear brother."

"Sister-in-law, why do you magnify trivial incidents?" Purna said and left the room.

# Chapter Eleven

Bhaskar usually came home at three in the afternoon, but it was six, and he was not home yet. Anxiety ruled since Rama Rao's scooter accident, more so with Malati. It was long after six o'clock when Bhaskar arrived.

"Why so late?" questioned Lalita at the door. Without answering his mother, Bhaskar winked at Malati, who was hiding behind the door. Malati replied with a smile. He walked in swinging his stethoscope, with Malati following him. *They are acting as if they are already married*, thought Lalita, *and he did not even answer me*. Lalita felt snubbed. Anger and envy raised their heads.

"Malati, find out if your *Bava* wants some coffee," Lalita snarled.

Purna understood the mockery.

"Yes, Aunt," Malati said and went in.

'Oh the queen has come; sit down," said Bhaskar as Malati entered the room.

"I was asked to inquire if you needed coffee."

"We had a party in the college. I have had coffee

and tiffin. You do not have to go for the coffee; sit down."

"When you were late, my heart almost stopped," she said as she sat down.

"*Hayyo!* Your heart stopping! Let's see," he placed the stethoscope over her heart and looked into her eyes.

"Your heart has not stopped but has sent me a message. Do you want to know what?" he teased.

"NO."

Lalita hurried into the room, and on seeing them, her blood boiled.

"What are you doing here when I asked you to inquire if he wanted coffee?" She could not hold back her anger.

"Mother, don't blame her. I asked her to sit. Can I not?" Bhaskar interrupted.

"Nothing wrong. You can ask her to sit, and you can ask her to lie down," she said and left the room.

Raja Rao lay in bed, reading a book in his room. Lalita writhed into the room, hissing like a wounded snake.

"I don't care what you say; Purna and Malati cannot stay in this house."

"Now, what?" Raja Rao asked, trying to be calm.

"What happened? You are asking calmly? Whatever needs to happen, has happened."

"Can't you tell me without riddles?"

"Whatever I say will be twisted and riddles for you."

"But what happened?"

"Your sister quarrels with the servants all the time. Your niece is showing her authority and bosses over everyone. They are quitting work. I cannot work. She should not work. What else?" she said furious.

"Why is she quarreling?"

"Why? Because that's her nature. Did she ever hire servants before? Or does she know how to make them work?"

"Here, Lalita, don't let your words flow." Raja Rao sat up from his bed, setting the book aside. Lalita remained silent.

"All that is being eaten and enjoyed is my father's money. Not your father's. The rights I have in this house are the same for my sister. My mother bore both of us for nine months and raised us. Just because she is a girl, I will not agree that she has no shade or standing in this house. If it was a younger brother instead of a sister, we would have given him his share. I have loved and respected you as a wife. I have never hurt you. I am only wishing for my sister's happiness," he said pointedly.

Lalita left the room. Purna overheard the conversation between her brother and sister-in-law. They were both bitter and furious. *She absolutely does not like me staying here*, she thought. *That Malati and I are unwelcome was distinctly said. That I quarreled with the servants! I don't know of any such sin! For my sake, brother is in a squeeze. Malati and Bhaskar's relationship is strongly entwined. Before this blooms into love, it has to be broken. That which can be dug out as a plant, has to be sawed off when it becomes a tree. It does not look like anyone in this house will have any peace unless we leave.*

Purna was unsettled after overhearing this conversation. She would inform her brother and move to another house. She was convinced of her decision. How to tell? What to tell? When to tell her brother?

She was unsure.

That night at dinner, conversation was cold. They ate whatever was served. Lalita did not inquire as to what anyone wanted or did not want. Purna tried to make polite conversation. Malati and Bhaskar were sitting across each other without a care, mooning at each other and giggling. That night, Raja Rao went to sleep, but Lalita was furious and hateful. Purna was restless. Malati was having sweet dreams.

# Chapter Twelve

Next morning, Bhaskar went to college as usual. Subbiah was in the veranda working on official business. Lalita created work for herself and did not come out of the kitchen. Purna came to the veranda towards Subbiah.

"Subbiah," she said softly. He stood upon seeing her.

"Please sit down," she said and sat next to him. "Subbiah, I want to look for an apartment and move out with Malati. Can you look for two rooms for us?" she appealed.

"That's no problem. I can do that. But did Ayya approve of this?"

"What can he say if I tell him that it is imperative that I move out?"

"Ayya has asked me to inquire about typing schools for Malati and bring the application forms. There is one school near the main hospital. Maybe I could look for a place close to that," Subbiah suggested.

"That's fine. A kitchen and a bedroom; I suppose there will be a small bathroom, too."

"Yes, Amma."

Everyone was quite cordial for two days. Subbiah rented a place with two rooms and an adjoining veranda. He wanted Purna to visit the place for approval.

"It is not necessary," Purna replied and gave him the advance and asked for a receipt for the same. She wanted to inform her brother and sister-in-law and move out as soon as possible. That evening, Subbiah brought the receipt for the advance.

"Where exactly is this place?" Purna asked.

"Across the hospital, there is a street leading to the bazaar. The typing school is beyond that."

Purna was distressed; her hand trembled as she took the receipt. *I hope I am not making a mistake,* she thought for a moment. *But if I stay in this house, there are bound to be hurts and misunderstandings. It is better I go.* She was determined.

Lalita had gone to the ladies' club; Raja Rao was supervising the gardener. Purna wanted to tell him about her plans. She sat in the chair on the veranda, waiting for him.

"Did Sister-in-law go to the club?" Raja Rao asked, joining her.

"Yes," replied Purna.

"Has Bhaskar not come back yet?"

"No."

There was a heavy silence. Raja Rao realized that Purna was perturbed.

"What, dear, you are out of sorts?"

"Nothing. What have you decided about Malati?"

"What is there to think about her? I have told Subbiah to inquire. It is about the typing school, is it not?"

"Yes, she does not seem to have any goal. She is reading story books and playing chess all the time and getting spoiled."

"I will ask Subbiah again."

There was silence for another few minutes.

"Brother," she said softly.

"Yes, dear," he said, taking a cigarette from his pocket.

"Nothing," she hesitated.

"Tell me what it is. Why this hesitation?" he said, drawing in from his cigarette.

"I have rented a small flat."

Raja Rao was shocked. "What? Is this house not big enough for you?"

"Well! How can this house not be adequate?"

"Then it means that you are not happy here."

"Don't say that, Brother. Who else do we have other than you?"

"Did you tell Sister-in-law?"

"It is only two days ago that I asked Subbiah to look for a place. He told me a few minutes ago that a place was available. He paid the advance and gave me the receipt," she mumbled.

"As you please," he said, offended.

Purna noticed the displeasure and unhappiness in his reaction. If she left without his approval, he may not help her in time of need. Her mind wavered, but staying was impossible, and she did not change her mind. Subbiah arrived, and Purna left in silence.

Malati was reading in the hall. Purna sat next to her.

"Look, Malati, we are leaving this house tomorrow

morning."

"Where to?" she said, disinterested.

"We are moving out. I found a place near the typing school."

"Why all this? Can we stay by ourselves?"

"If God has given me loneliness, there is nothing we can do about it," Purna stated and left the room.

Malati's heart was hit by a stone. She did not like leaving this house. If she left from here, she would be separated from *Bava*. Her heart was heavy and sad. She did not know that the sweet thoughts in her heart today were the beginnings of love. She seemed to have been enlightened. Her heart questioned her, "Do you know why you are sad? And why you are hurt? Her heart told her loud and clear the reason for her sorrow. You are in love with Bava! You are devoted to him like to God. Malati put her book aside and went to her mother and saw her packing.

"So! When are we leaving?"

"Tomorrow morning after lunch," Purna said dryly.

"Why are you in such a hurry? What were we lacking here?"

"We are not lacking anything, here. In fact, we have too much here."

"You and your thoughts," Malati accused.

"We are moving for your sake. The typing school is close by."

 Malati did not reply.

Lalita returned from the club. Raja Rao, who was in the veranda, apprised her that Purna was in the process of moving to her own apartment. Her happiness reached the skies. She congratulated herself on her wishes being granted. But she pretended to be shocked, as she wanted to conceal her happiness. She was bubbling with joy to be rid of them from the house. She would break not one, but four coconuts to the Gods. She made every attempt to conceal the joy from her face and went in.

"What is this, Purna! When your brother told me this out of the blue, I wondered. This is too much. You have already packed your bags!" She showed surprise.

"We plan to leave tomorrow morning."

"Your brother told me that you have found a new apartment as you want to leave, but he did not say that you are leaving tomorrow in a hurry. Does he know about it?"

"I did not tell him, but I was about to. Just then Subbiah arrived, and I came inside," she said.

"I thought we would all stay together and not live separately. When your brother told me about it, I could not believe it."

"What is there to believe or not to believe? I thought it would be close to Malati's typing school, and so I made this decision."

"As you please," she said and left the room.

Malati heard the sound of the scooter and knew that Bhaskar had arrived. Bhaskar spoke to his father at the entrance and came inside and saw Malati standing near the door. He walked into his aunt's room.

"What? I hear that you are leaving and that you have found a new place?" he said stunned.

"Yes, dear," she said in a low voice.

"Good. Very good. This house is not big enough for you," he said, disappointed.

"Don't say that," she murmured. Purna could not speak further.

"Auntie, your leaving is not a good idea."

"Malati is getting bored here."

He looked at Malati, who was in tears. The tears were pouring down her cheeks. Bhaskar was overwhelmed. He went into the kitchen looking for his mother.

"They are going to another house?" Bhaskar said on seeing her.

"Yes, they are going. No matter how much we care, they still consider this a stranger's house. Your aunt decided in an instant and is determined."

"Couldn't you tell her?"

"When did she look for the house? When did she decide to go? I have no idea. She told your father this evening after all the arrangements were made, and he in turn told me when I returned from the club."

"If you protest firmly, she may listen to you."

"If she did not listen to your father, why will she listen to you or me?" Lalita said helplessly.

"Did you see Malati? She is full of tears."

*If her eyes are full of tears, I will give her a towel to wipe them*, she thought spitefully.

Everyone was present at dinner.

"When exactly are you leaving?" asked Raja Rao.

"She says tomorrow morning," Lalita joined in.

Raja Rao remained silent.

Lalita thought that her husband would force his sister not to leave, just as he coerced her to leave Madras and come here. Raja Rao recollected the few bad incidents that occurred in the house and did not stop Purna. The night was spent peacefully. The next day being Sunday, Bhaskar was home.

Purna and Malati were to leave after lunch. Nobody spoke much at the dining table.

"By the way, where is your new apartment?" asked Raja Rao.

"It is in the street across the main hospital," replied Purna.

"If it is close to the hospital, Bhaskar can meet you whenever he can."

Lalita startled at her husband's words.

"Take whatever you need from here," Raja Rao added.

"All right," said Purna.

They all rose after lunch.

"Go at three o'clock, after your coffee," said Raja Rao and left the room.

Purna packed her bags; Malati looked around and went into the hall. She picked up Bava's photo and hid it between the pleats of her sari and placed it in her bag between the clothes. *After we leave, Aunt will probably raise a hullabaloo and suspect everyone else. The frame is of silver and would cost about a hundred rupees. I will face the consequences later. I want that photo. It does not concern me who is blamed for this,* she said to ease her conscience.

At lunch, Bhaskar noticed that Malati was worried. Later he went to the door of her room and said, "Come here."

Both went towards the garden, and there Malati expressed her sorrow in loud tones.

"Quiet! Your house is close to the hospital, and as soon as I finish my work, I will come straight to you. Is that all right?"

She nodded her head to mean, "Yes."

He wiped her tears and lifted her face. "Why these tears now? I said I would visit you. Didn't I?"

"My tears are not stopping," she said, laughing.

He drew her close to him. Just at that moment, Lalita came out to the veranda and saw them.

"Bhaskar!" she said, agitated.

"Coming, Mother."

Malati walked behind him. Lalita looked at the culprits sternly. She wanted to correct Malati but swallowed her anger.

"Coffee is ready," she said and went in. The car was at the front, and the bags were loaded. Everyone had their coffee. Purna and Malati touched the feet of Lalita and Raja Rao in bidding good-bye.

"Subbiah, you also accompany them and drop them off," said Raja Rao. Everyone sat in the car with grim faces. Purna shook her head to mean, "See you later." Malati looked as if she was going to the sacrificial altar. Raja Rao, Lalita, and Bhaskar stood there watching the car drive out the gate.

"Everyone could have stayed together, but you created differences of Us and Them," said Raja Rao with sadness.

"Who created differences? Maybe she did not have any freedom here," said Lalita sarcastically.

"Bhaskar, their house is close to the hospital. Keep checking on them frequently. I will also do that," said Raja Rao.

*I have not got rid of this nuisance completely,* thought Lalita.

As soon as the car reached the gate, Purna told the driver, "Stop at the bazaar, as I have to buy some utensils and groceries."

"Buy? Why you could have brought some from the house. There are plenty of utensils there," said Subbiah.

"Oh! I made a mistake. I wanted to ask Sister-in-law about them, but I forgot. She did give me some pickles, as I am moving to a new place," said Purna cleverly.

Subbiah was smart enough to guess the depth of truth in those words.

He was not unaware of the feelings deep down within the members of the family. When he saw the utensils shop, he had the driver stop the car. Purna bought whatever she needed, and Subbiah loaded them in the car. Malati did not get down but sat in the car. "Why should we go to another place with all these inconveniences?" She was quite unenthusiastic about the whole matter. Purna went next door and bought broomsticks and matches and other sundries in small packets. They reached the new apartment. Malati and Purna walked in, while Subbiah and the driver unloaded the car.

"What kind of house is this?" said Malati sulking.

"Appropriate for the rent," replied Purna.

"You should have seen the place before paying the advance," Subbiah said, contrite.

"Don't worry, Subbiah; we are used to living in such houses. After seeing Uncle's bungalow, Malati does not like anything else."

"It will take a month to clean up this place," said Malati in a critical tone.

"I can do it in two days," said Purna determinedly.

Shall I send the servant from the house? He will clean up the place," said Subbiah.

"No, I can manage this little place," said Purna.

"You don't have any bed or mattress for tonight," moaned Subbiah.

"We will manage for tonight. If you can come tomorrow, we can buy some."

"All right," Subbiah said and left.

Subbiah returned home after dropping them. He informed Raja Rao that Purna had bought groceries and utensils, and that they did not have any beds.

"Lalita did you hear? You should have inquired about all that," Raja Rao barked.

"She went in a hurry, and I did not think about it," said Lalita defensively.

Raja Rao respected Lalita in every way. He did not let her be in want of anything. But when he was angry, Lalita trembled. Raja Rao, unhappy that his sister left the house, could not bear the fact that she was suffering there.

"Subbiah, load two cots and mattresses, a dining table, and four chairs into a cart and take it there. I will also come."

Lalita watched, paralyzed.

# Chapter Thirteen

Purna lit the stove and made some rice. With the yogurt she bought at the store and the pickle given by Lalita, she served Malati dinner on an aluminum plate and did the same for herself. She felt as if released from prison. Malati, however, was sick at heart. Malati opened the door when she heard a knock. "Amma! Uncle has come."

"Why?" Purna went out of the kitchen. The car was parked in front, and behind it was a wooden cart loaded with cots, bedding, a table and chairs, and other things. Like a magician, Subbiah arranged everything in the house. Was this a dream or God Vishnu's magic? Purna and Malati were amazed.

"Can I come in?" said Raja Rao with great pride at his major accomplishment.

"Brother, how can I forget your kindness?" Purna said gratefully.

"I did not do anything," he said, patting her on the back. Both their eyes were moist. Raja Rao and Subbiah left soon after.

"Uncle is kind," Malati said.

Purna wiped her tears. Subbiah informed her that the bank accounts and insurance money would take a while in getting transferred.

Raja Rao was ruminating on his way home.

"They need witnesses and certificates, as this was an 'accident' case. They have to be convinced that she is the true beneficiary," said Raja Rao.

"Yes, that is why the delay," added Subbiah.

"It may take some time. She will not open her mouth and ask. She is hesitant. She has the strength to face anything that comes her way. That is why God is giving her all these difficulties," he said sadly.

Subbiah did not reply.

Lalita sat in the veranda quite confused after giving Subbiah and her husband all that they wanted to take. Bhaskar freshened up and sat next to his mother in another chair.

"Why did Aunt have to go in such a hurry without thinking of the pros and cons?" said Bhaskar starting the topic.

"I don't understand her ways," said Lalita, feeling liberated.

"Malati did not like to leave here at all," said Bhaskar.

Lalita stayed quiet for a moment and said, "You have to study well for your exams. Father has a lot of hopes on you."

"What are those hopes?" he asked mockingly.

"That you go for higher studies and that you become a famous doctor."

Subbiah and Raja Rao returned.

"You are back so soon?" Lalita asked.

"We went, unloaded the car, settled them, and came

back. House is quite small."

Raja Rao went in. Subbiah was ill at ease.

"Ayya thinks the house is small, but for that rent I could not get a bigger place."

"Never mind," Lalita said, perversely satisfied. She went inside.

# Chapter Fourteen

The following day, Bhaskar left the hospital after work, stopped at a hotel for some coffee, and went straight to Purna's house. He rode the scooter down the street next to the hospital. He saw a woman standing outside a house and asked, "Yesterday my people moved into a new place; can you tell me where that is?"

"Oh! That house! Some furniture also arrived last night. That's it." She pointed to a house two doors away.

"Thanks," he said and walked ahead. He saw a number on the door, which was faded and scratched. He looked carefully and saw the number thirty-nine. He stopped in front of the house, locked his scooter, and took a small packet from his attaché at the back of the scooter. He went to the door, which was ajar, pushed it open, and found Malati sweeping cobwebs from the wall with a long broom in hand. Her saree was tucked up. He came from behind and gave her a hug.

She jerked. "Who is this?"

"Who is it? Who else can it be?" he said, teasing.

"Bava, your hands have a hospital smell."

"Not hospital smell, lotion smell."

"Amma! See who has come!" Malati yelled.

"Who is it? Bhaskar?" She came out of the kitchen, wiping her face with the edge of her saree.

"Are you coming straight from the hospital?" she asked affectionately.

"Yes, Auntie."

"How about your lunch?"

"I had some coffee at the hotel."

"How can that be? I will bring you some tiffin," she said and went inside.

"Amma, tiffin now and dinner later," said Malati.

"Oh, sure," replied Purna from the kitchen.

Malati took the broom inside while Purna brought out the coffee.

"Amma, you said, 'Why do we need a table and chairs; now you see why. Bava does not sit on the floor to eat."

"Drink this coffee; I will bring the tiffin later," said Purna.

"I don't need any tiffin. We can have an early dinner," Bhaskar said.

"Sure."

"See what I brought for you." Bhaskar handed Malati the packet he had brought.

"Is it a chess board?" she asked, wide-eyed, receiving the packet.

She opened it. "It is new!" she said enthusiastically.

"My first present to you has to be new. How can I give you an old one?" he said with pride.

"Shall we play?" She swayed her head.

"Sure, why should we give up our routine?"

"That's fine." Malati was bubbling.

Bhaskar drank his coffee and set the cup aside. They placed the board on the table and set the pieces. They had started the game when Subbiah entered and handed her the papers from the typing school.

"Thanks, Subbiah garu. Where is the typing school?" asked Malati.

"Close by, as soon as you cross the main road."

Purna called out to Subbiah from the kitchen. He went in and found Purna sitting in a chair. She pulled the edge of her saree over her shoulders. "I am finding it difficult for money." Purna sounded distressed.

"This is not a matter of transfer. Since Rama Rao garu died suddenly, it is an accident case. There is need for certificates and witnesses; that is why the delay," he said, weighted down.

"Then I am in a bind," she said, afraid.

"Amma, when God has blessed you with a brother who will grant your every wish, why should you worry?" he said laughing.

"Subbiah, what is it that you are not aware of? Though there are only three in the family, they will have their own expenditure. It does not look good for me to stretch my hand out for money frequently."

"What are you saying? When did you ask frequently? The day you moved, you bought kitchenware, and brother was very unhappy."

"Yes, I am his life since childhood," she said, sighing.

"I am not ignorant of that fact; I also grew up with you," he said humbly.

"Don't mention this to brother, but please see that those papers get taken care of soon," she appealed.

"Yes, I will see to it," he said and stepped out.

"Subbiah, are you going home?" asked Bhaskar.

"Yes, I am going home. Do you have any work for me?"

"No, nothing."

Subbiah left.

Bhaskar and Malati continued playing, sometimes arguing and sometimes giggling.

"Dinner is ready, Have you finished your game?" shouted Purna.

"We have played two games. That's enough for today," said Malati rising.

"She lost both the games, which is why she wants to stop," Bhaskar said loudly so that Purna could hear.

"Hey! No, I did not lose," Malati protested.

They cleared the table of the chess board, and Malati set up plates and glasses for dinner. Malati and Bhaskar were joking and laughing throughout the meal.

"You both eat; I will eat later in the kitchen," Purna said.

"It is getting dark; I had better go, Auntie." Bhaskar shook his head at Malati, bidding her farewell. She went up to the door to see him off and sat down to peruse her papers from the typing school.

"Amma, I have to pay the typing school."

"Sure, we can pay them," she said, serving herself some rice.

The next morning at nine, Malati took out her saree that was ironed and got ready.

"I will go to the typing school to see where it is and if I can, will pay them. Can you spare me fifteen rupees?"

"Where is the school?"

"I don't know. Subbiah said I have to cross the main road."

"Go and see where it is. If you like the place, give them these ten rupees, and we will pay the balance later," Purna said, handing her a ten-rupee note.

"Close the door. I am leaving," said Malati as she bounced out the door.

Purna finished all the chores in the kitchen and was anxiously waiting for Malati to return. "They said the school was close by; why is she taking so long?" she thought. It had been an hour and a half since she'd left.

Malati arrived. "It is ten rupees a month, and the admission fee is five rupees. The school is not very far," she said, enthused.

"When do you have to start?"

"I will go tomorrow. It is from three to four in the afternoon. I paid them."

Purna felt a little relieved that Malati had joined the typing school. *Once she has the certificate in hand, she can get any office job. How long can I be selling gold jewelry, and how long will the cash in hand last? I have to manage somehow.*

They both had lunch. That evening, Bhaskar came straight from work. Purna placed a plate of semolina *upma* and coffee in front of him.

"Thanks very much. I did not go to the hotel today."

"I knew it," she said, laughing.

"Where is Malati?" he asked.

"She is washing up."

Malati came, wiping her face with the towel, looked at him, and smiled. She went back in, braided her hair, placed the bindi on her forehead, and pulled up a chair and sat next to him. He had just finished his coffee.

"Where are you dressed up to go?"

"For a stroll with you," she said seductively.

"You want to go out with me! Let's go," he said.

"Where to?" she queried, squinting her eyes.

"To the beach. We'll go early and come back soon."

"It is still hot."

"Amma, Bhaskar and I are headed to the beach," she said, and the next minute they were gone.

*Malati is being indiscreet,* thought Purna. *Wonder what will happen if they keep going around together? Wonder what danger is in store? Malati grew up between her father and grandfather's grandiose pampering for fifteen years. Along with her naughtiness, she grew up stubborn. She listens to me only if she wants to, and most times not.*

Bhaskar was riding towards the beach, with Malati riding in the rear seat.

"Why do you go dancing on the roads?" said Malati, afraid.

"Why? Are you scared? I won't have an accident like your father. If you are scared, hold on to my waist."

She clasped his waist with both hands. Swinging and swaying, they reached the beach. They walked through the sand, stood on the shore, and saw the waves without blinking.

"What are you looking at?" she asked.

"Did you see the waves?" he said.

"Yes, I did."

"What do you think when you see them?"

"When the ocean is overflowing, it is scary."

"Let's sit awhile." They sat on the sand. Bhaskar did not say anything and looked straight at the sea.

"What are you thinking?" she said.

"The exams are coming near. This year I have the theory and the practicals. I should study carefully. Already my father and mother think that I am wasting my time playing chess. We have to stop our escapades for a while," he said decisively.

"Some days means how many days?"

"Not days, but months."

"So you won't come for a few months?" She was dismayed.

"After my exams and after the results, I will convince my parents and take you home as my lawfully wedded wife," he said and looked at her tenderly. He took her hand in his. Their hearts spoke in that silence. Malati's heart was filled with happiness. His was filled with her. They spent a few sweet moments.

"Bava, shall we go?" she murmured.

"All right," he said. They got up and shook the sand from their hands and clothes. Swinging their clutched hands, they left the ocean behind them.

By this time, Purna had finished her cooking and laid the table. The three of them sat at the table, with Purna serving them.

"I forgot the ghee." Purna rose.

"I will get it," Malati said and went into the kitchen.

Stuttering for words, Purna told Bhaskar, "If you don't mind, I will tell you something."

He was mixing his rice and looked up, wondering what it could be.

"It is not good to play with a girl's life, dear. Malati is of marriageable age." She sounded hurt.

Bhaskar completed her sentence. "And this marriageable Bava will marry. Auntie, if I ever marry, it will only be Malati. I will not marry anyone else. I swear to you," he said boldly, stressing every word.

Purna trembled at these words.

"Bhaskar, don't make such major promises. You are both young. You are not able to understand the joys and sorrows of life. Even so, I wonder what your mother will say tomorrow."

"WE are getting married, not my mother," he said firmly. Malati returned with the ghee container and placed it on the table. The three of them ate their dinner.

The weather was not smooth.

"I'll be leaving," he said, looking at Malati with a smile.

Malati was bursting with happiness, while Purna was nervous.

# Chapter Fifteen

Bhaskar went home. Both his parents were in the hall, presuming that he went to Purna's place. Lalita asked a leading question like a lawyer. "Is everyone all right in Aunt's house?"

"Yes I had my dinner there," Bhaskar said as he walked in.

"Aunt's cooking must be very tasty," said Raja Rao.

"Food is not the tasty part," said Lalita with a sting.

"Don't make unwarranted statements. Where did he go? He went to my sister's house."

Both were in their own thoughts for a few minutes.

"Let's go eat," Lalita said and got up with a sigh.

*Those unlucky souls left the house, but they are still stuck like grease. The situation has gotten out of control. I will make my attempts. I will find obstacles to curtail the circumstances.* Lalita was determined that as far as she could help it, Malati and Bhaskar would be separated.

Subbiah was in the veranda writing. She called him pleasantly.

"Yes, Amma," he said standing up.

"When you get a chance, please go to Purna's house

and inform Purnamma that I would like to talk to her and that she should come over," she said and went inside in a huff.

Subbiah suspected trouble. These days Lalita was like the incarnation of Sage Durvasa in a woman's form. There was going to be a great Mahabharata war. He was amused. The next day he visited Purna and gave her the message that her sister-in-law would like to meet her. He also gave her the money and passbook from the bank and informed her that the accounts from Madras were transferred, but the insurance money had not yet arrived.

Purna could not imagine why her sister-in-law wanted to meet her. Wild thoughts filled her head, and her heart raced.

*When I go, then I'll know*, she told herself. The next day after she finished her household chores, she changed her saree and got on the road. She checked to see if she had small change and hailed a cycle rickshaw. Since she got a ride, she reached her destination quickly. She paid the fare at the gate and entered the driveway gingerly.

"Is Amma garu at home?" she asked Chukamma, who was standing in front of the house.

"Yes, she is in her room," she said and led her inside with Purna following.

"Ammagaru, Purnamma has come."

"Purna, come on in. Come." Lalita sat up in bed. "Did you forget us after you went away?" Lalita taunted.

"What are you saying? I just got busy."

"Chukamma, bring us some coffee," Lalita said.

"When Subbiah told me that you wanted to see

me, I got scared. Is everything all right?"

"Yes, we are all fine," she replied in a hateful tone. "Is Subbiah taking care of your money matters carefully?"

"Oh, yes, I tell him what I need, and he takes care of it prudently. Whatever, he is a gentleman."

"You are always looking ahead; have you thought of Malati's future, like marriage?"

Chukamma brought the coffee. Purna thought that she was going to finalize plans for Bhaskar and Malati's wedding. Purna brightened, but suppressed her happiness.

"When both parents are alive, getting a girl married is not easy. How can I, single, get a girl married? It would be a task as big as a yagna," Purna reproached.

"Take your coffee; it will get cold," Lalita said and handed over one glass to Purna and took the other for herself. Both drank and left the empty glasses on the table.

"Purna, I want to tell you one thing; don't misunderstand," said Lalita.

"What is it?" Purna was nervous.

"It seems my son and Malati are wandering in the bazaar. If one person says it, I wouldn't believe it, but if four people comment, I have to. He is a man. Tomorrow he will marry another girl. But she is a girl; what will happen to her? I thought you did not know about this, and therefore, I sent for you to inform you. What will be her future? She will be in the streets. I know you will feel bad on hearing this, but I had to let you know. I don't know. They play chess in the house. What is this wandering in the bazaar?"

"When I go home, I will give her a good scolding," said Purna in anger.

"Don't be so severe; tell her gently."

Lalita went to her almirah and took out a long brown cover and gave it to Purna.

"What is this?" Purna was perplexed.

"This is one thousand rupees. You and Malati leave town, and go far away from us. This is best for both of us."

"Sister-in-law, you are older than me. You are like my mother, and I will not refuse you, even if it is inconvenient for us. If it is the best for you, we will definitely leave."

Not able to contain her sorrow, Purna covered her face with the edge of her saree. She composed herself in five minutes and rose.

"I shall go now," Purna said, leaving the brown envelope on the bed.

*I have lit the fire,* thought Lalita. *There will be a fire let me see who is going to get burned.*

# Chapter Sixteen

Purna reached home fuming and furious. Malati had just arrived from her class. Purna looked at her with disdain.

"Why? Why are you looking at me like that?" Malati went away in a huff. They ate dinner in silence. Even when Malati tried to accost her mother, she answered in anger. Both of them did not sleep that night.

"Amma, why are you unhappy? Can't you tell me?" Malati asked, unable to restrain herself.

"If it is not sorrow, is this happiness?" was the reply.

"Are you in want of money?"

"Not only money; everything is a bother," Purna said rudely. Malati was quiet. Purna was flooded with Lalita's words.

*She wanted Malati to leave town,* she thought. *She is looking for a large dowry and a basketful of gold. More than the sons, mothers have the greed. Bhaskar promised that he would not marry anyone else except Malati. Why is God testing me like this? If I was alone, I would have fallen into a well. How can I be rid of the responsibility of this pathetic life of Malati?* Purna suffered in silence.

After a while she composed herself and curbed her bad thoughts. No money in hand, she had to somehow get money by tomorrow. She should not touch the money in the bank. *I will pawn my gold bangles and get some money. When I get the insurance money, I will retrieve them. I will never ask Brother. When there is no support from the lady of the house, it is better to beg than to ask from that house.*

The morning sun rose. There was no conversation between mother and daughter. In the evening, Malati went to class as usual. Bhaskar visited in the evening.

"Sit down; I will bring you some coffee," Purna said.

"Auntie, I thought that Malati and I would go to the hotel. Where's she?"

"Malati just returned from class and must be washing her face. Bhaskar, I need to talk to you about something," she said seriously.

"What is it?" He sat in the chair that was his customary place.

"Bhaskar," she said hesitatingly. "You are young, at an age for falling in love, the age of indignation, and ignorant that the world is a bad place. You have said that you will marry Malati. Until the formalities are over, can't you stay away from each other?"

"Aunt, why are you suspicious? Our lives have been tied together long ago," he said convincingly.

Malati entered. "Bava has come already," she said happily.

"I came for you. I thought I would take you to a good hotel."

"I am ready." She left the book on the table and said, "Amma, we are leaving." Gurgling with laughter, Malati left with Bhaskar.

Malati returned from school quite late that day. Purna was stunned. She was shaking with nervousness. Sister-in-law ordered that they cannot live in town, scolded her, and advised her to keep Malati under control, all in no uncertain terms. *But Bhaskar says their lives are already knotted. How will I bow to this predicament?* Purna was miserable. *"Oh God!"*

She remembered that she had work in the kitchen. She finished what she needed to do and went to the bedroom. Next to the timepiece in the almirah she saw Bhaskar's photo in the silver frame and was taken aback. "This used to be on the table in the hall in Brother's house. How did it come here? Did Bhaskar give it to Malati, or how else could it come here?"

Malati was sitting in the rear seat of the scooter with both her hands tightly around Bhaskar's waist. They reached the hotel without talking. Malati got down, and he parked the scooter and locked it. They entered the hotel but saw no vacant table. A server boy strolled by and informed them that a table would be ready very soon and to please wait. They waited at the entrance. Soon a table was available, and the boy cleared the dishes and wiped it clean. Malati and Bhaskar sat at the table, and the server boy came back and asked for their order.

"Pakodis and coffee for me," said Bhaskar to the boy, and looking at Malati, "What do you want?"

"Same?" she said.

"No sweets?" asked the boy.

"Do you want any sweet?" Bhaskar asked Malati.

"If you want—" she said, dragging her words.

"No, I don't want."

"Then I also don't want."

"There are fresh *jangris* made today," said the boy, who made it sound mouth-watering.

"All right, get us two."

The boy left. Bhaskar leaned the chair back and stretched himself. Malati was looking at the couple at the adjacent table.

"Why are you looking at that couple?"

"Look, they are newly married."

"They may be thinking the same of us."

Malati blushed. The server brought two plates of *jangri* and two spoons.

"Why spoons for jangri?" Malati asked.

"There are some brave men who eat *chekodis* with a spoon."

Malati laughed.

"Your mother is getting jittery; I wonder why?" Bhaskar became serious.

"Elders are very suspicious," Malati said.

"They are worldly wise and experienced; that is why they get suspicious."

The boy brought fresh *pakodis* and coffee and placed them on the table.

"Green chili pakodi!" he said, chewing on one.

"Bava, if you are going to vanish until after the exams, I feel bad," Malati said, narrowing her eyes.

"You have to work hard to achieve your goals. We have to make small sacrifices now. What do you say?"

"Whatever you say," she said innocently.

Bhaskar sipped at his coffee. Malati also had her coffee but was pensive.

As the place was getting noisy, they paid the bill at the manager's desk and stepped out on to the road.

"Where to from here?" he asked.

"Let's go home," she said.

"I have to buy some notebooks at the shop nearby. Let's go," he said, taking her hand.

Sweet sensations touched her hand. *If the rest of our lives are spent holding hands, how wonderful it would be!* Wishful thoughts were shining inside her. They went to the bookshop, where a wrinkled old man was sitting at the far end.

"What do you need?" he asked, rising from his chair.

"Notebooks," said Bhaskar. The old man pulled out a variety of notebooks. Bhaskar set aside a few from the lot. "I will take these," he said and pulled out a ten-rupee note. The old man placed the books in a paper bag and handed him the change.

"Where to from here?"

"Shall we go to the beach?" Bhaskar asked.

"Wherever you want to go."

They went to the beach and walked in the sand and sat down buoyant.

"I put the notebooks in the pouch of the scooter; I hope nobody takes them," he wondered.

"Why will they take them?" She was carefree.

For a few minutes, they looked at the sea.

"By the way, did you tell your parents about us?" she asked shyly.

"Let my exams be over, and I will tell them then."

"How much longer for your exams to be over?"

"It will be a few months. I have to study well."

Malati was disappointed.

"Why are you so sad? Are you worried that I am not studying well?"

"No, not that. It is dark. Let's go home."

They reached home, and he dropped her off at the

door.

Malati walked in gleaming.

Purna was in the kitchen, and Malati called out, "Amma," and went in.

"Where all did you wander around?" asked Purna sternly.

Malati knew that her mother disapproved.

"We went to the hotel and later to buy notebooks. We went to the beach for a short while," she said softly.

"There is Bhaskar's photo in the room. It used to be in the hall in Uncle's house. How did it get here?" Purna asked.

Malati's face was blank.

"Why don't you talk?" she asked again.

"Bava gave me," she said, without a quiver.

"Malati, your aunt does not want to make you her daughter-in-law, and tomorrow if Bhaskar listens to his parents, your Bava slips out of your life. Then, what is your fate?"

"I trust his promises. After that, it is my destiny. Whatever is written for me will happen." She was bold and confident.

Absorbed in their thoughts, Malati and Purna went to bed without dinner. Both of them could not sleep, and both did not talk to each other until dawn.

# Chapter Seventeen

The next day, keeping to her routine, Malati went for class at three in the afternoon. Purna was struggling for money. She took one of her gold bangles to the bazaar. There she visited two or three jewelry stores and settled on one of the bigger ones. The shop owner was sitting on a mattress with a box in front of him. He did not look very old. He was fair, heavy-set, and had dark, curly hair. His lips were stained red with *paan*. He was wearing a white pajama and *jubba* and looking suave. The walls had multicolored pictures of Sri Venkateshwara, Vighneswara, Shiva Parvati, Lakshmi, and Saraswati. Incense was burning in front of the Gods.

On seeing Purna, the shopkeeper said, "Come in," very reverentially.

"Sir, pawn this bangle and give me six hundred rupees," she pleaded, giving him the bangle. He scratched the bangle and studied it, took out a small scale from the box in front of him, and weighed it.

"I cannot give you six hundred, but I can give you four."

She thought for a moment. "All right, let it be so." He counted four hundred rupee notes and gave them to her. She took the receipt that had her name on it. Purna's mother gave her extra gold at the time of her wedding, and Purna was thankful. Today it came in handy. She came home, locked up the money, and waited for her daughter. The day was a little hot and Purna was tired. She rested her back on the bed for a while.

She heard noises at the door and opened the door for Malati.

"Malu, I brought money today. Tomorrow you can pay whatever fees that need be paid," she said.

"Where did you get it from? Did you go to the bank?"

"No, these days gold prices are soaring to the skies. I pawned one of my gold bangles."

"How much did they give you?"

"Four hundred only. They say price of gold is going high, but I got only four hundred. I did not sell it," she explained.

"How do you plan to bring it back?" Malati asked anxiously.

"The insurance money will be coming soon, and when it comes, I can redeem it."

"When the money comes, I will buy four voile sarees. I do not have proper sarees to wear to class."

"Let the money come. We will see. You can take two of my good sarees; I don't need them."

"You only have two, and I am not going to take them," Malati retorted.

# Chapter Eighteen

A few months passed by without incident. Malati was attending classes. She was happy lost in sweet dreams. In a month she would be getting her certificate. When she got her certificate, she could join any office as a typist and make a living. With her added income, it would be as different as hot and cold water. Purna was looking forward to that day when she could live respectably anywhere. Still her heart was not satisfied. Brother and Sister-in-law were not visiting her. Even Bhaskar stopped coming. Subbiah also was scarce in his visits. Whoever did or did not come, she missed Bhaskar's visits. She was baffled. His parents must have prohibited him from coming here. She was sad and unhappy.

Malati returned from class and was concerned about what was bothering her mother and decided to ask her.

"Amma, why are you always lost in thought?"

"Nothing. Bhaskar is not coming here these days. Maybe he is not feeling well."

"No, nothing of that sort. He is studying for his

exams. He said that he wouldn't come until they are over. It is not easy studying medicine," she said proudly, as if she were the one studying.

Malati's words consoled Purna.

Malati had no classes to attend the following day. She was very chirpy. It was nine o'clock in the morning.

"I think I will wash my hair today," Malati said.

"Sure, do that. I will go to the bazaar," Purna said and left with her bag.

Malati undid her braid and went to the almirah where she had Bhaskar's photo and looked him straight in the eye.

"I lied that you gave me this photo. If anyone at any time asks you, you are not going to let me down, are you?" she asked him in the photo.

She heard a knock at the door and thought, *Amma must have come back, as she forgot to take her money. She does that all the time.* Malati opened the door. Bhaskar was standing there with a big smile.

"Bava!" she exclaimed, ecstatic.

"You did not expect me to be here, did you?" Bhaskar walked in.

"No, not expecting to see you for a few months, I have been miserable."

"I wanted to see if you were suffering or not. How can I stay without seeing you?"

"Good," she said excitedly.

"Mother not home?"

"No. She has gone to the bazaar. Last time, after you dropped me home, mother gave me a good thrashing."

"Why?" he said, shocked.

"Why? Come here, I will tell you," she said and went to the bedroom. He followed her. "Here, this is your photo."

"How did this come here?" He was astonished.

"How did you come here? The photo came the same way!"

"How did I come? Mother was very unhappy that the photo was missing. She suspected all the servants and yelled at them."

"I knew that she would suspect everyone in the house. I needed this photo. I brought it the day I came to this house."

"You are a thief."

"Aren't you also a thief? You have stolen my heart."

"What about you?" he joined in her verve.

Malati held his face and put her arms around his neck. They swayed and fell on the bed nearby, and he hugged her close to his heart.

"Bava, what is the matter today? You are very possessed."

"That's the way it is," he said and drew her closer.

She tried to wriggle herself out but cooperated with him. She was engulfed by him and crushed in his arms. They crossed barriers. Love took over, and they were lost in each other.

"I'm scared," she said.

"Don't you trust me?" He got closer in an embrace.

"Don't say that. If I don't trust you, who can I trust?"

He closed her mouth in a tight embrace and stopped her from speaking any more.

Rustling was heard at the door, and Malati opened it. Purna had returned from the bazaar. Bhaskar came out of the room.

"When did YOU come?" she said, not very pleased.

"A little while ago," he said casually.

Both of their hair was disheveled, and the bed sheet was crumpled. Purna was leery, but controlled her temper.

"I will be going," he told Purna. He looked at Malati and left.

"Malati, you are crossing your limits. I have been telling you, but you don't care for what I say. Aunt does not like your marrying him at all. She is looking for riches and dowry. And you, you are playing out the familiarities of marriage." Purna glowered with unbridled fury.

Malati was silent, acknowledging guilt. There was a brief silence.

"He said as soon as the exams are over, he is making wedding arrangements," Malati replied, feeling wretched.

"I don't know what he will do. There are still a few months more for the exams. But you are making many mistakes." She swiftly took the packets of groceries into the kitchen.

Bhaskar did not come back again. Malati presumed that he was immersed in his studies. She was going to school as usual.

"As soon as the exams are over, I have to talk about wedding plans." Purna was firm in her decision.

# Chapter Nineteen

Days, weeks, and months went by. One day, Malati felt nauseous and threw up. Purna was thunderstruck. She was trembling with fright. After throwing up and washing her face, Malati lay on the bed.

"What have you done?" Purna wailed.

Malati did not speak. She closed her eyes and lay still in bed. Purna was looking out of the window into space. Malati opened her eyes and saw her frightened mother at the window.

"Amma," she called softly. The mother turned around to see Malati's eyes, shining with tears.

"What is the use of anything now?" said the mother.

Malati sat up in bed. "I have made a mistake."

"All these things need to be thought out before, not after," said Purna, sighing.

"What do we do now?"

"What else? We will go to the doctor."

"No, I will meet Bava and tell him about it."

"What will he do?" the mother said loudly.

"I don't know."

"I don't know is not an answer. You cannot push it

aside; you have to come to some decision." Purna was abrupt.

"We will meet Bava and do whatever he says." Malati gathered courage.

Purna did not reply.

"I won't go to school today," said Malati.

"We can think about school later."

"It is now seven thirty. About eight he will be going to the hospital or college. Before that I will go to Uncle's house and meet him." Malati braced herself.

Purna did not like Malati to go to her brother's house.

"Shall I go?" Malati asked.

"All right, go. Let's see," Purna muttered.

Malati brushed her hair, changed her saree, and left.

"Your eyes are red, so wash your face before you go," said the mother.

"If it gets late he won't be home. I am going."

Malati stopped a rickshaw on the road and got into it. She reached her uncle's house with trepidation. The rickshaw stopped at the gate, and she went in. Chukkamma was at the door, and Malati asked her, "Is Amma garu home?"

"Yes, she's home. Have you forgotten us, or have you forgotten the way to our house?" she said incisively.

"We are trifle even to Chukamma," Malati thought.

Chukkamma and Malati reached Lalita's room. Chukkamma went inside and came out in two minutes. "Amma wants you to come in."

Malati entered her aunt's room with apprehension.

"Why, dear, why have you come this way so early in the morning?" Lalita said cordially.

Malati sat in the chair nearby. Lalita noticed the

dejection in Malati's face.

"Is everyone fine?"

"Yes," she replied in a low voice.

There was silence for a few minutes.

"Sit down." Malati was hesitant.

"Auntie," she said, confused. Lalita looked her straight in the eye. "Is Bava at home?"

"Why?" she said raising her tentacles.

"I have to talk to him."

Lalita's anger rose in her.

"What do you want to talk to him about?" She was agitated.

"An important matter."

"He is having exams now. There is no need to chat with him on important matters."

"Then I will come back again." Malati got up.

"Having come, stay a while."

Malati was frightened and sat down.

"May I know what this important matter is?" Lalita asked sharply.

Malati was wavering.

"Why? Why are you thinking? Is it something that I should not know?" Lalita gave a sting.

"That's not it," Malati replied, puzzled.

"Then, what is it?" Lalita spoke a little louder.

"I am—" Malati stopped. Lalita eagerly awaited the rest of the sentence.

"I am going to be a mother," she said boldly.

"What!" Lalita was perturbed.

"Yes, Auntie," she said shyly and bent her head.

"Does your mother know about this matter?"

"Yes, she knows."

"So what did she say?"

"She wanted me to tell Bava."

"You are real cunning people. You wander around town, and you want to frame Bhaskar for this sin."

This time it was Malati's turn to be indignant.

"Aunt, I can swear to God."

"Talk softly. There are servants in the house who can hear. It will not look good. Now you don't go after Bhaskar. Let him live with honor and respect."

"Aunt, if you say that—what about me?" Malati fell at Lalita's feet, but Lalita pushed her away with her foot.

"These days, for a seat in the medical college, they pay one lakh. After he completes the course and becomes a doctor—you want to get him for free? Is this your mother's motive? You can't get cheaper than that. That innocent boy, and you want to catch him. Is this your conspiracy?" she roared.

Malati opened her mouth but closed it without saying anything.

"I am not one to fall for these lies. Fifteen days after her husband dies, she packs up and lands up here, single. I knew then alone that you had ulterior motives. Now I know. Here it is. I am telling you for the last time. Don't claim a relationship of uncle and aunt and come here again."

"I swear to God, this is the truth. You can ask Bava if you wish."

"Who wants you to swear? Empty promises. What do you want me to ask him? Do not try to contact your uncle or Bhaskar. Do you hear?"

"Then what about me?" Malati pleaded.

"When you were wandering around town did you ask for my permission? Ask your useless mother who could not keep you in control. GO."

Malati got up and stood like a statue.

"Why? Why are you still standing?"

Malati could not speak another word. With tears pouring down her face, she put the edge of her saree in her mouth and recoiled out the door. After Malati left, Lalita was dispirited. She came out of the room and jolted on seeing Chukkamma standing there at the door. She was afraid that Chukkamma might have heard every word of the conversation.

"Did you hear everything?" she asked sternly.

"Yes, I did. It is really strange," said Chukamma, surprised.

"To fulfill their wishes, people can go to any length, as long as they are not ashamed. 'If you can give up an ant's worth of shame, you can gain the whole world,' was not said in vain."

Lalita went back to her room, full of resentment, and lay down. The snake that is wrapped around your foot will surely bite. This snake needs a big blow. She contemplated her next move. This should not be told to Bhaskar or her husband. *If they knew, there would be a wedding this very moment. Anyway, the plan that these low lives have made should not be accomplished. It has to be broken. That's it. She wants to see Bava. That shameless face. Why could her mother not have come? If our gold is good, they will surely want—Bhaskar also has joined them. He gave them all the opportunities.*

Malati returned home in the rickshaw. As soon as Purna opened the door, Malati burst into tears. Purna understood that the mission was a failure.

"Did you meet Bava?" she asked.

"No."

"Wasn't he home?"

"I don't know."

"What does that mean?" Purna was perplexed.

"I met Aunt, and she told me in definite terms that I should not meet Bhaskar or Uncle. She cursed both of us with unmentionable names. She said that we want to bag him without a dowry, that's why we came to town," Malati said, sobbing and wiping her tears.

Purna's sorrow knew no bounds. All the words spoken by her sister-in-law were killing, but one had to yield to circumstances. That was her lot. Her self-respect took a big blow, but the mistake was hers.

"What shall we do?" Purna said.

"When the exams are over, Bava will come, and I will tell him."

Purna covered her shoulders with her saree and went into the kitchen.

Two days dragged by, and in the confusion, Malati did not go to the typing school. Purna did not ask "why."

# Chapter Twenty

Lalita thought for two days and came to a decision. She wrote to Purna. She read it twice and made some corrections. She changed her mind, tore it up, and wrote another and read it again and was pleased.

At any cost, this drama of the mother and daughter had to be foiled. If she could curse them like the sages of yore, she would have. She read the letter over again and placed it in an envelope, pasted it and went to the veranda, looking for Subbiah. The guy who came faithfully each day and took care of matters did not come that day. So she grimaced and went to the gate and shouted for the driver. "What happened to Subbiah? He has not come yet?"

'He said that he had some work at home and told Ayya that he would be late," the driver replied.

"The day I have work for him is the same day he has work at home," Lalita went in grumbling.

As soon as he arrived, Subbiah said, "Amma, did you need me?"

"Subbiah, take this letter and give it to Purna," she said, coming out of her room.

"As you wish," he said and took the letter.

Purna's heart was racing in many directions. Her thoughts were torturing her. *This unexpected monster has fallen on me. How do I get out of this situation?*

Subbiah went later in the morning and noted the misery on Purna's face.

"Amma, what happened?" he burst out.

"Nothing. Whatever happens every day," she said diplomatically.

"Is that all!" he was relieved.

"Amma garu wanted me to give you this letter," he said and handed over the envelope. Purna's quaking hand took the letter. Subbiah noticed the tremor.

"Amma, you are not well. Go to the doctor and get examined," he said with concern.

"Yes, I will," she said and concluded the conversation.

"These are your bank papers and passbook. All the money has been credited. The insurance money also has come. Another policy of about two thousand rupees is still to come. That will also arrive soon. I will visit you off and on. Whenever you need, I can bring you cash from the bank. I shall take your leave."

"All right, Subbiah."

"Should I tell Amma anything?"

"There is nothing to tell," Purna groaned.

As soon as Subbiah left, Malati came out of the room.

"What is this letter?" she asked.

"Aunt sent it."

Purna opened the envelope, removed the letter, unfolded it, and read it.

*Chiranjeevi Purna,*

*Blessings.*

*I am feeling bad that I have to write to you like this. Malati came here the other day and dropped a thunderbolt. I confronted Bhaskar, and he said that he knows of no such sin and was amazed that Malati could accuse him of a horrible crime! How could she do this to him? He was very much hurt and disgusted. If your brother knows about all this, the respect and status he has for you will go into mud. I cannot imagine how hurt he would be. So I have decided not to tell him about it. We will be blessed if the two of you could leave town. What else can I write? Did I ever think that our relationship would break up like this?*

*That's all. Bye.*

*Lalita*

Malati, who stood nearby, not only noticed the expressions but also the tears flowing down her mother's face. Purna read the letter and, wiping her tears, gave it to Malati.

Malati read the letter with a rapid heart.

"Mother, there is something foul here. Bava is not that kind."

"All men are like that. They will use every opportunity and then ditch you," said Purna, repulsed.

"Among men, aren't there any good ones? I will not take any decision without meeting him," said Malati firmly.

"So you think Aunt is lying?"

"I don't know," she said, doubting.

"Because of us, they have lost their respect and status in society. What else can Bava say or do? It is better if we leave town. We'll go to the twin cities

Hyderabad where no one knows us."

Malati, much defeated by the letter and her mother's words, understood that leaving town was for the best, but she wanted to write at least one letter to Bava.

*Bava,*
*Greetings.*
*I came to your house to tell you of an important matter. Aunt was angry and said that I could not see you, as you were busy studying for exams. But Bava, I have to tell you a very important matter. Please come home once. I am not going for classes. I look forward to seeing you. I hope you will definitely come.*
*Your Malati*

"Amma, I have written a letter to Bava to come. I will drop it in the mail.

"What did you write?"

"I asked him to come home one time."

"We'll see when he comes," Purna said dejectedly.

"When he comes, we will ask, 'How can you say that you do not know anything?' On top of it, he was disgusted." Malati was outraged.

"First let him come," said the mother.

Purna did not expect that Bhaskar would come. Lalita would have her son in her clutches.

Lalita was suspicious when a letter arrived in her son's name. She thought for a moment as to who it could be from. *What does it matter? I will read it. That devil must have made her daughter write.* She cursed Purna. She opened the letter, and as long as she was reading it, took frequent sighs. Having read it, she tore it to pieces. *I have to be careful in the future. I don't know how many more letters will be arriving.* She took another long, deep sigh.

Malati waited a week for Bava to read the letter and come to her, but he did not come. Disheartened and listless, she wrote again and again.

*Bava,*
*Greetings.*
*I wrote you a letter, and I hoped that you would come, but you did not. In a week's time, we are leaving town. I did not think that you were a cheat. I may be far from you, but you are not far from me. Your spirit is growing within me. One day we will meet, and that day I shall stand up and face you.*
*I am not writing this with ink but with my tears.*
*That's all.*
*Malati*

Malati did not tell her mother about the second letter. She dropped it in the mail. But Purna noticed everything. Lalita watched out for another letter in her son's name. She got one as expected and opened it. She was elated that her son was having a child. She hesitated to tear up the letter and thought for a moment. Shall I reveal this secret? But I have told Purna to leave town. If I reveal this secret, not only will I lose a handsome dowry, I will also lose respect, honor, and standing in the community. Lalita tore up the letter.

# Chapter Twenty-one

The next day Purna made her travel arrangements. She sold the bangle that she had pawned and got more money. She packed the utensils in a gunny bag. She put all the clothes in the box. She left the beds and mattresses and locked the room. She wrote a letter to her brother and gave it to her neighbor with instructions that she give the letter and keys to anyone who came from her brother's house. Even though she tried hard to reduce her belongings, she collected ten pieces of luggage. Purna and Malati left in two rickshaws, reached the railway station, settled all the stuff above and below the berth, and sat down. It was a three-tier ladies' compartment, and everyone was cramped. Malati sat near the window and her mother across from her. Their faces were jaded.

"Why doesn't the train leave?" said Malati, fed up with the wait. When the guard waved the green flag, she sighed with relief.

"Where should we stay in Hyderabad? What is our future?' Purna sat stupefied and did not want to think about it. The train gathered speed slowly, and Purna's head was bobbing in unison. After a half hour of the train's departure, the ticket collector came by. He stood in front of each passenger, inspected the ticket, and tore the lower half of the ticket given to him. When he came to Purna, she gestured for him to ask Malati, who took two tickets out of her purse. She took some time to take out the tickets, as she was day dreaming. Having got this opportunity, the ticket collector looked at the luscious figure without blinking.

"Are you going to Hyderabad?" He was voracious.

Malati nodded. Purna thought that beauty in a girl is a handicap. Her neighbor looked at Malati and said, "Your daughter?"

"Yes," Purna said dryly.

"Is she married?"

"No." Purna was peeved.

"You have family in Hyderabad?"

"Yes."

Purna wished that it would be the end of the conversation.

"Where do they stay?" the lady asked.

Purna did not answer. *Why is she asking me questions like a lawyer in a courtroom?* She was touchy. All the others ate the food brought in carriers and were settling down to sleep. Malati and Purna starved all night. They did not even drink the coffee they brought in a flask or the tiffin in the bag. Malati, sitting by the window, looked out. Purna sat with her eyes closed, her head resting on the berth.

The next morning the train chuffed into Nampally Station, tooting its horn.

Even before the train could come to a stop, the coolies got onto the railings of the train, and as soon as it came to a stop, they entered the compartments and started picking up luggage. The passengers alighted, and their luggage filled the platform. Everything was disorderly. Purna could not think straight with the coolies shoving and pushing. Purna and Malati got down but asked, "Where do we go?" The train unloaded its contents very quickly, and the coolies carried luggage and headed to the exit. Purna found a coolie to carry their luggage and went along with him, with Malati following. They piled the luggage into one auto. Purna and Malati sat in the other. "Where to?" asked the auto driver.

"Are there any charity shelters?" Purna asked.

"I don't know of any," he replied.

"Are there any nursing homes?"

"Yes, there are."

"Then take us there," Purna said.

Malati looked at her mother, wondering why a nursing home.

The auto accelerated away. The roads were uneven, and Purna and Malati were bouncing. Some of the roads were unpaved.

*Why are the roads like this in a big city?* thought Malati.

The auto stopped at a nursing home in Himayatnagar. Purna entered through the gate. There was a man sitting at a desk in the front veranda. Purna stood at the door. He looked up and asked, "Did you need anything?"

"This is not our town. We just arrived. Are there any rooms for rent?"

"This is a nursing home, not a hotel. There are two rooms for the convenience of the relatives of patients to stay, not for rent," he said impatiently.

"If you can let us stay in a room for two days, we will find some other room and leave. We do not know anyone in town," she said distressed.

"How many of you?" he asked.

"Not too many, just me and my daughter," she implored.

"Since you do not know anybody here, you can stay in one room. I am just the manager here. I need the doctor's permission for this. He will come at five o'clock in the evening. You can ask him, but don't tell him I said so."

Purna thanked him and emptied the autos. The room was very dusty, and Malati sat near the door.

"You stay here," said Purna. She went to the hotel across the street and brought two packets of food. They sat at the entrance of the room and ate. There was a water pump in the garden, and they drank water, cupping their palms. They washed their faces and wiped them with the edge of their sarees. One young man coming through the gate stopped them and politely asked, "Who are you?"

"We arrived this morning. The doctor will be coming in the evening at five, and until then, the manager told us that we could stay in this room."

"All right, I will get the room cleaned."

A few minutes later, a woman swept and dusted the room. Purna waited for the doctor, sitting at the doorstep, while Malati slept on the bed. Purna saw the doctor entering the nursing home at five o'clock. She followed him and stood in front of him, greeting him with folded palms.

"Yes, dear, what do you want?" he asked kindly.

"Doctor, my daughter needs an exam."

"What's the matter?"

"No disease; I think she may be pregnant."

"The lady doctor will come in the morning, and you can see her tomorrow."

"We are staying in this room, and we need your permission to stay there."

"No problem, you can stay there. I will tell the manager."

Purna put her palms together in gratitude. There is no God better than a kind man.

"The lady doctor will come in the morning," Purna told Malati, who took a deep sigh. After the meal from the hotel that morning, they did not have any water, either.

"Shall I bring a carrier of food from the hotel?" Purna asked.

"I don't want anything. You can bring for yourself," said Malati, disinterested.

"What do you mean, you don't want?" Purna went to the hotel and returned in half an hour with food for the two of them in the carrier. She separated the containers and served both of them in a platter. After eating, they washed their hands at the pump. After the train journey and the mental stress, they both laid their backs down on the cots. Neither could sleep. The night passed. Next morning Purna went to the pump, and having washed up, again went to the hotel with her carrier, this time taking a flask along and returning with two cups of coffee. After seeing the coffee, Malati got out of bed, washed up near the pump, and sat next to her mother. They looked at each other with mournful eyes and drank coffee in silence.

"By the time the doctor comes, comb your hair. Have a bath before everyone wakes up. I will have a bath after you are done," the mother said.

Without a word, Malati bathed, combed her hair, and braided it and placed a bindi on her forehead. Purna also got ready and waited for the doctor. The lady doctor came at the appointed time and went into her room. On seeing her, Purna and Malati went to the adjacent building, which was the nursing home. Malati was nervous. A couple of women went in to see the doctor. *They are probably old patients,* thought Purna. When they came out, the *dayi* asked Malati to go in. Both of them entered the room and sat in front of the doctor, who asked Malati what the problem was. Malati looked at her mother.

"She missed a period," Purna said in a low voice.

The doctor then took some papers from the shelf and wrote down some details about Malati: age, etc. When she asked for the husband's name, Malati said, "Bhaskar," quite unhesitatingly. After examining her, the doctor confirmed that Malati was indeed pregnant. When the doctor pronounced the fact, Purna felt lightning hit her. It was only a suspicion all this while. There was a chance that it might not be a pregnancy, but now all hope was shattered.

"We are poor and are not in a state to raise another life," Purna entreated.

The doctor looked at Purna and said, "I understand what you are telling me. She is advanced in her pregnancy, and if you are unable to raise the child, they will take care of it."

Purna was confused. The doctor wrote out a prescription.

"Take these medicines that I have written. The girl's health is good. Come back after one month," she said and rang the bell on the table. On hearing the bell, the *dayi* entered. Purna and Malati were still standing.

"You can leave," said the doctor.

Both of them came out of the room altered. Purna leaned against the wall, crushed, and did not know what to do and which direction to turn. Malati sat on the bed, her face vacant. You could not find any thoughts even if you searched for them. Whether suffering or looking for a decision, no one could guess.

"We have to wait a few more months. I wonder if we can stay in this room." Malati broke the silence.

"I will enquire with the manager about that."

"I wonder how much rent we need to pay for this room."

"I will find out. If they say ten or fifteen, then we have to pay it."

"Can we afford it?"

"I do not want to take you anywhere else in this condition," said Purna, heaving.

In the meantime, the disgruntled manager went to his office. Once he settled down at the desk, Purna entered his office.

"Did you get to see the doctor?" he asked, fumbling for the desk keys in his pocket.

"Yes, she did, and he also said that we could stay in that room."

"Yes, the doctor mentioned it to me."

"We saw the lady doctor today, and we are new to this town. We may have to stay for a few months. I hope you have no objection to that," she supplicated.

"The room rent is seven rupees a day. As long as you

pay, there will be no objection. You can use a stove but not any coal burners."

"That's fine." Purna was content.

Malati anxiously awaited her mother's return. "What did the manager say?"

"If we pay the rent, they have no objection. We can stay as long as we want. We just cannot use a coal burner. The rent is only seven rupees."

*How much trouble Amma is taking on my behalf! Solving all the problems that arise from this.* Malati took a deep sigh.

Purna cooked on the stove whenever she could, and when she was tired, she would bring a meal from the hotel. Days and months were going by. She did not buy the medicines written by the doctor, but Malati was quite healthy.

Malati had also changed. There was no naughtiness left in her. Circumstances made her patient and tolerant. Malati and Purna stayed in one room, but their thoughts were not evident to each other. Different thoughts were running in their heads.

*I had many dreams I loved Bava, honored him, and still respect him. After marriage I wanted to mold according to his wishes. I trusted him. I surrendered to him. I was hasty. Mother warned me. I cannot even guess what the future is going to be. Will I not see him some day? I will definitely ask him, 'Is there so much treachery in you?' When I see him I will hand over his child to him. Let me see how he can disown me and our child. Because of me, mother is suffering and crumbling.*

This is Mother's love.

*Malati went beyond boundaries. I should have known that Sister-in-law would never make Malati her daughter-in-law. I should have punished Malati. Who is marrying these days without a dowry and lots of gifts? Bhaskar is going to be a doctor. It is normal if she is looking for a big dowry. She wrote that she did not think that the relationship would break like this. As good as saying, 'Never step into my house.' We left town without informing them. Brother may be thinking that I am untrustworthy. Let that be. Malati has been victimized. Will this remain a secret?* Such thoughts taunted Purna.

# Chapter Twenty-two

One morning, at eight o'clock, a young boy riding a bicycle asked, "Is this Raja Rao's residence?"

Subbiah, who was at the entrance, said, "Yes, this is it."

"This evening Raja Rao's childhood friend Seshagiri Rao would like to come and visit and wants to know if he will be home."

Subbiah went in and encountered Lalita in the hallway.

"Amma, one Seshagiri Rao, who was Ayya's childhood friend, wants to come and visit him this evening. A boy has come to enquire if it is convenient."

"*Emandi*, your childhood friend Seshagiri Rao wants to meet you this evening. He sent a young boy to find out if it is convenient for you. Can he come?" Lalita yelled out.

"Seshagiri Rao, my childhood friend, who is that?" Raja Rao muttered to himself.

"What does it matter who he is? Are you going to be home or not?"

"Yes, tell them I will be home."

Subbiah conveyed the message to the boy.

"Who is this Seshagiri Rao? Why is he visiting you now?" Lalita entered her room, thinking aloud.

"I think that he was in school with me. Seshagiri Rao. Hmm. I discontinued my studies, and he went on to higher education. I hear he is a professor at the local university. If it is the same person, our fathers used to be good friends. His father had a large family, and Seshagiri is the oldest. When he was in school with me, he was the one who would come first in all the subjects. When I was faring badly in my studies, and he could not pull me up, he would say, 'Education is only to make money. Why do you need an education? You have plenty of money.' My father put an end to my education. Since Seshagiri Rao's father could not afford it, my father gave him monetary help and encouraged him to further his son's education."

"I don't think so. Beggars are better off than these teachers," said the all-knowing Lalita.

"He is not a school teacher; he is a university professor."

"I don't know about all that. These people are always having dilemmas. His daughter's wedding, or son's education, or an old mother's illness. He probably needs money and is digging up his childhood friendship. As if he does not know that you live in town. Anyone would laugh at it. There is a big board on the main road and that big shop with all the neon lights. You listen to me."

"What is it I have to hear?"

"This childhood friend of yours, if he talks about money, refuse him in no uncertain terms. When he asks about money, do not have a face like a question mark. Don't embarrass me and look at me."

"Is that all? Please stay inside so I don't look at you."

In the evening, Raja Rao waited for Seshagiri Rao at the entrance, when an auto stopped at the front gate. He was accompanied by his brother, Gopala Rao. They unlatched the gate and walked in. He was not in dearth of brothers and sisters. His father supplied him with plenty before he died.

"Hey Seshagiri, how long is it since we met?" Raja Rao accosted him walking towards the gate.

"I did not know that you are in this town. When my wife got sick, we went to the hospital. There, a young man was talking to the doctor. He was handsome. I wondered who he was, and the people around told me that the handsome boy is your son."

Raja Rao patted Seshagiri's back with pride.

"They also gave me your home address. You did well by putting your son into medicine. If your son is a doctor, you don't have to search for medicines or doctors," he said approvingly.

"I do not have an education, which is a major flaw. You can make a lot of money in business. But the respect and worth that you receive with an education, that distinction you do not get with money. What do you say?"

"You can ask my wife; she will say, 'What job is this?'" said Seshagiri Rao. "But nowadays it isn't too bad. Professors are given decent salaries."

Raja Rao served tea to Seshagiri Rao and his brother.

'Why all this? You have taken a lot of trouble," said Seshagiri Rao accepting a plate of snacks.

"My childhood friend, you are visiting me. How can

I not even give some coffee?" said Raja Rao smiling.

"You have not lost your mischievousness. When I knew you were in town, I had to visit you."

"Your coming to our house is a festival."

"What affection! When we were young we used to dig at each other," Seshagiri Rao reminisced, looking at his brother. They placed the empty glasses and plates on the table. Looking toward the interior of the house," Raja Rao yelled," Lalita did you order any *paan*?"

"I will get it now," answered a female voice from inside.

"There is no need. We do not have the habit of *paan*, so you need not order them. Actually we came here—" Seshagiri Rao paused.

Raja Rao's heart raced. I hope he does not bankrupt me and ask for a loan of thousands.

"I have a daughter. She is in first year BSc. I thought that we could strengthen our childhood friendship with another relationship. I came here to let you know about this. Whenever convenient, if you, your wife, and son could visit us, it would be good, and you can meet my daughter."

Raja Rao's heart slowed down. "You said you do not have the habit of paan; how about cigarettes?" Raja Rao stood up and pulled some cigarettes from his pocket.

"No, not even that."

"You are lucky. However much I try, I am not able to give up this habit," said Raja Rao as he lighted a cigarette.

"Let us know before you come over to see the girl," Seshagiri Rao said, going back to the topic of marriage.

"These days you only create and raise children.

After that, it is their decision. Isn't that so?" said Raja Rao, inhaling the cigarette.

"Yes, that's true. But I thought before you agree to someone else that I would mention my daughter, so you can keep her also in mind when you are choosing a daughter-in-law."

"I cannot promise. My son might say, 'I have already promised.'"

Everyone had a laugh, and Seshagiri and Gopal rose from their seats.

"Raju, can you call for an auto for us?" Seshagiri Rao said.

"Subbiah!" Raja Rao yelled.

"Yes, sir," said Subbiah.

"Drop them home in the car. You also accompany them."

"Why car? Get us an auto," said Seshagiri Rao.

"You hold it. I am the father of the groom. You are forgetting that," Raja Rao joked.

Everyone laughed. The car was brought, and Seshagiri Rao, Gopal Rao, and Subbiah left in the car.

"Have they gone?" said Lalita, crouching from inside, having overheard the whole conversation.

"Yes, they have gone. He wants our Bhaskar to marry his daughter."

"Who wants this wretched alliance? What do they have for us to marry into? He studied on your father's charity."

"Whether they have money or not, Bhaskar is the one getting married. Not you or me. Ask him what he thinks." Raja Rao was clear about the terms.

"How can I? He does not stay home at all for anything."

# Chapter Twenty-three

Bhaskar studied day and night diligently and with determination. He wrote all his exams well. Today were the practicals and the last day of exams. It was six o'clock in the morning. It was ages since he met Malati. *I must see her today,* he thought. He rolled in bed and looked at his watch. *I have practicals today, and it is already six.* He got out of bed with a start, finished his bath in a flash, and went into the dining room with a spring in his step. Everything was set on the table. Lalita and Chukamma were standing there.

"I just want some hot coffee and nothing else," said Bhaskar.

"Why? Son, aren't you going to eat something?" Lalita oozed with affection.

"It is late. Has my scooter been brought out?"

"Why, scooter? You say you are late, so take the car."

"Father may need the car; I'll take the scooter," he said and drank his coffee.

Bhaskar went straight to the hospital. The other candidates were discussing some cases. The veranda was noisy and in confusion. Students in groups were turning the pages of their books with fervor.

The practicals were over, and Bhaskar did reasonably well. He answered the questions about his case to his satisfaction. He was anxious to meet Malati. Some of the candidates were rehashing their cases. He was not interested in a post mortem, and he went to his scooter. "Greetings, sir," he said to the professor who passed by.

*It has been a long time since I've seen Malati. I am going to spend the rest of the day with her. I should have informed at home that I will be coming late. If I go home now, it will delay me. I'll go to the hotel and to Malati.* Bhaskar sped away on his scooter. He reached the hotel and parked the scooter after locking it. The hotel had filled up with his college mates. He sat down at an empty table.

"What can I get you?" asked the waiter coming to the table.

"Coffee," he said. Exhausted from the exams, he placed both his elbows on the table and covered his eyes with his hands. The coffee arrived, and he woke up to the rustling.

"Don't you want any tiffin?" asked the boy.

"What do you have?"

The boy recited, like his multiplication tables, a page-long list of items. He started with the fresh pakodas made daily and ended with the laddus made the day before.

"Did you want me to bring you anything?"

Bhaskar nodded sideways to mean "No." He finished his coffee, paid the manager, and headed to Purna's house with exuberance. Now that the exams were over, he felt liberated from prison. Sweet thoughts swayed in his head, and his face became radiant. When he reached Purna's house, he saw a big padlock on the door. He got a jolt. "Where could they have gone after locking the door?" The neighborhood kids surrounded his scooter. He was informed that Malati and Purna vacated the house. The neighbors next door had gone for a movie. Unnerved, he reached home. Lalita was happy to see him.

"Amma, Aunt and Malati have vacated and left the place." He was over-wrought as he got down from the scooter.

"*Hayyo*! What is this?" Lalita's heart was beating fast, such that someone needed to hold it down.

"Does Father know anything about this?"

"I don't know; he did not tell me anything."

Bhaskar was in anguish. Lalita looked at him with sympathy but was unable to carry on a conversation with him. She was tongue-tied.

"Is Father home?"

"No."

Bhaskar went into his room.

From the moment Purna sent the letter through Subbiah, Lalita wondered if she made a mistake and what the consequences would be. She was jittery. But she was relieved that Malati and Purna had left town. And Chukkamma, who saw Malati's coming and overheard the conversation, had to be silenced. It is only then that she could see the fruit of her labors. She called out to Chukkamma.

"Whenever we have festivals I have only been giving you money as a bonus, but I have not bought you a saree at all. How many months have you been watching over us? This time for the approaching big festival, buy yourself a saree to your liking," Lalita said.

"How can you say that, Amma? What is it that you have not given me? You have been very gracious. As you wish, I will buy a saree for myself."

Just then Raja Rao alighted from the car accompanied by Subbiah. Chukkamma went in.

"Why are you sitting there scared? Did Bhaskar not come home?" Raja Rao sat down next to her.

"Yes, he did."

"Did he do well in the exams?"

"I don't know; he did not talk about his exams but gave me other news," Lalita stammered.

"What is that?" he said surprised.

"Purna and Malati vacated their rooms and left."

Raja Rao got up, shaken.

"Why?" he said, when he regained his voice.

"Bhaskar!" he yelled.

Bhaskar came out.

"What? Aunt and Malati have gone?"

"I went to Aunt's house, and it was locked. The neighbors said that she had vacated and left."

"What is she thinking? Where could they have gone? Why did they go? I hope she has not left town. I do not know; she does not open her heart to me."

Subbiah said, "I will go and enquire."

"I will also come," said Raja Rao. "Let's go." The two went back into the car. They reached Purna's house in minutes.

The next-door neighbors had returned from the movies, and the light was shining through the window. Raja Rao got down from the car and knocked at the door. A little girl opened the door and, on seeing him, ran inside.

The house owner came to the door. "Greetings," he said. Raja Rao joined his hands together in response but did not say anything. The man brought out two chairs, and they sat down.

"My sister Purna and her daughter were living in the place next door. I heard that she vacated and left. I came to find out whether she told your family anything about where she was going," said Raja Rao.

"I was not in town. When I returned, I heard about it. I don't think they told my family about where they were going. They gave the keys and a letter to be given to you. Daughter!" he yelled.

The little girl came and stared at Raja Rao.

"Ask mother for the letter and keys."

She returned with the same. The anxious Raja Rao received them and opened the envelope hastily, took out the letter, and read it. He was wan.

*Dearest Brother,*

*Greetings. I hope you will forgive me. I am leaving town as I cannot face the circumstances. I don't know what God's will is. I hope that we will meet somewhere sometime.*

*My respects to you and Sister-in-law. My blessings to Bhaskar.*

*Your sister,*
*Purna*

On reading the letter, Raja Rao was paralyzed. He still did not know about the circumstances. What is it that she could not face? He could not think of any answers. He was confused. He wiped his tears and got up.

"I'll take your leave. I will send my man to empty the rooms in a few days," he said and joined his hands together to bid goodbye. He got into the car, saddened, and went straight home. Lalita sat in the veranda, filled with dread.

"Here, Purna gave these keys and a letter for us. The neighbors gave it to me," he said and handed them over to her.

Lalita startled when she heard there was a letter. She read the letter and was glad that nothing in the letter was incriminating or hateful. *Purna is a large-hearted woman.*

Raja Rao, head bent and confused, walked up and down.

'Did you read the letter?" he asked his wife.

"Yes."

"Why did she go? Where did she go? She did not write about it. She could not face the circumstances. I wonder what they are," he said listless.

Subbiah, shocked, stood still.

"Subbiah, take the keys and arrange for a cart and empty the house. Ask if there are any other dues to be paid."

"Yes, sir," he said and took the keys.

After a while, Raja Rao, Lalita, and Bhaskar sat down to dinner in silence.

"It is surprising. Where could the two of them have gone?" said Raja Rao.

"Maybe her father-in-law was sick and she got a letter," said Lalita.

'What do I know?" her husband said irritably.

Bhaskar was silent and vanquished. Lalita looked guilty and sheepish. She was the one who asked them to leave, so as to separate Malati and Bhaskar. She was able to chase them out of town. She now realized that she could not chase Malati out of Bhaskar's heart. Bhaskar rose without finishing his dinner.

# Chapter Twenty-four

The days were dragging, and Bhaskar did not have his mind on anything. Getting out of his room had become scarce. When Lalita looked at him, she was afraid that he would lose his mind. And her husband, he was maimed. If she talked to him, he would fall on her like a tornado. His sister was his life. If she did not say a word to him before leaving, he was not able to figure out what the reason could be. What was this horrible circumstance that she had to face? Raja Rao wasted away in these thoughts. Sick with worry, Raja Rao had no sleep at night and no food during the day.

If he only knew that she was the one to have chased them out, would he forgive her? What fault did she find in Malati? What could happen if she became the daughter-in-law of the house? What would have been wrong? Both Bhaskar and her husband had an especially favorable opinion about Malati. If they knew where the two of them were, they would fall at their feet, beg for forgiveness, and coerce them to come home. But where were they? What happened to them? All she wanted was an alliance for her son where there would be a lot of money; anything wrong in that? Lalita was bewildered.

One day Subbiah brought back all the chairs and tables and said that there were no pending dues.

# Chapter Twenty-five

The exam results were released. The medical college was in a furor. Bhaskar graduated with many prizes. His friends and even his enemies were congratulating him. His parents were overflowing with happiness. The college arranged a grand celebration for all the graduates. After the dinner, the principal and other professors delivered their speeches. Bhaskar, the winner of many prizes, received applause and congratulations. He thanked them all in a few words. The graduates came forward and announced their future plans. Some were going to set up practice in town, some others were going for higher studies. A few were going to the villages to serve the rural poor. They wanted to know what Bhaskar's plans were. He said that he was going to stay in Vizag by joining the government service.

After the speeches were over, the people dispersed and were locating their vehicles. Bhaskar unlocked his scooter and was about to ascend when he heard his name called from behind. He turned around to find his classmate Sarojini standing at a distance.

"I wanted to specially congratulate you," she said

softly.

"Thanks," he said curtly.

"I even wanted to garland you, but hesitated as you may not like it."

"Why garlands?"

"They wear garlands during weddings," she giggled.

At that, Bhaskar was thrown off guard; he looked at her intensely for a moment and rode away on his scooter. She was puzzled and followed him to the beach in her car. Bhaskar sat in the spot where he and Malati had sat, as this was a sacred place. *Malati left without informing me. Where have they gone? Why have they gone? Aunt has a tender heart.* He thought that Malati would write to him, but he was disappointed.

He heard a voice from behind. "What are you thinking?" It was Sarojini.

He turned around and wondered, *Why is she following me like this?* He was annoyed.

"Oh, you!" he said.

"Yes, me," she said modestly.

They did not know what else to say. She thought that he would ask her to sit beside him. After standing for a while, she sat at a distance and watched him, but his eyes were far away into the ocean.

"Do you come here every day?" she asked, starting a conversation.

"Whenever I can," he said abruptly.

"You are a nature lover, are you?"

"Yes. There is no beauty in anything else other than nature."

"That means you are capable of loving."

"Yes, God gave that gift to all humans."

"Do you love only nature? Do you not love persons?"

He was pensive. "Why won't I love?" he said profoundly.

"Who are those lucky ones?"

"My parents."

She was amazed. "Love for parents is mixed with respect," she responded quickly.

"If you do not respect, how can you love?"

She was unable to express her true feelings. He noticed the distress on her face.

"I'll be going," he said and rose.

"Will you be coming here tomorrow?" she asked, also rising.

"I don't know. I can't tell about tomorrow, today."

"Is that all?" she said disappointed.

# Chapter Twenty-six

Months passed by in confusion and a daze. The doctor took good care of Malati, who delivered a bouncing boy with ease. One fine morning when Purna was sitting on a bench outside the delivery room, the ayah came bustling out and said, "Purnamma garu, you have a grandson. He weighs six and a half pounds. He is fair, like the mother."

"Grandson!" Purna felt a burden.

After a half hour, Malati was shifted to another room. The ayah laid the child next to the mother. Purna stood near the door and called out to Malati, who looked towards her.

"How are you, my dear?"

"Fine, Amma," she said weakly.

She wanted to know Malati's opinion about the child. "Can we raise this child?"

"If we do not raise our child, who else will raise him?" Malati exclaimed.

Purna was considering giving the child away to an orphanage, but on hearing Malati's reaction, did not think about it again.

She went close to the baby. "He is just like my brother," Purna said mournfully.

"Why? He looks like his grandpa," said Malati cheerfully.

"You are tired; you'd better rest," said Purna.

She went back to her room, had a bath, and ate some boiled vegetables. There had been enough expenditure until now. She had to make permanent living arrangements. *One small room should be sufficient,* she thought. *We cannot afford more than that. I don't know what else God has in store for me! This is life. Sufferings cannot be escaped.*

She gathered up courage and started looking for a place to stay. Within four or five days she found a place in an old building close to the nursing home. There was a veranda next to the room. She could fix up the place by hanging a mat on the veranda to be used as a kitchen. She gave an advance to them and came back to the home and visited Malati, who gave her a bill that she received from the manager for some hundreds.

"I did not think it would be this expensive," said Malati sadly.

"Don't worry. I have taken a small room for rent. We'll go there and straighten everything out." Purna was brave.

Malati looked at her mother with gratitude for all her struggles. That look moved Purna's heart. The next morning Purna sat in a rickshaw and went to Abid Road. There were many jewelry shops with glass-covered shelves filled with gold and silverware. There were gold chains hanging and many shiny bangles and rings. The man at the counter looked like the owner.

He was weighing a gold chain on a small scale for
a customer. After weighing the chain, he placed it in
a small velvet-lined box. After they left, he accosted
Purna.

"What do you need?" he asked politely.

"I want to sell this chain," she said and gave him a
gold chain.

He took it and rubbed it against a stone in two
places and weighed it and perused it. It was an antique
with the kind of unique workmanship not available
these days. It was fairly heavy. He was satisfied and
gave Purna four thousand and odd in rupee notes.
Purna put them carefully in her purse and got into the
rickshaw. She stopped at a clothes shop. She bought
clothes for her grandson and went back to the nursing
home. She settled them in her box and visited Malati,
who was fast asleep. She returned to the room and
thought of the morrow. Malati and child would have
to come to this room, so she cleaned it and, being too
tired to cook any dinner, drank some milk and went to
sleep exhausted.

# Chapter Twenty-seven

It was morning, and Purna hurried as Malati would be waiting. She sat on the bed as the baby boy slept in the adjacent cradle. As the cool breeze would affect the new mother, Purna wrapped Malati's head with a scarf and took her back to the living quarters. She came back and wrapped the baby and took him to Malati and laid him next to her. She went again to the home and emptied the room. She waited for the clerk to pay all the bills. He usually came at ten o'clock, but today he was late. It was eleven o'clock, and she got tired of waiting. He finally came at the gate, cursing, then entered the room muttering and sat at his desk. Purna also entered the room.

"What, are you leaving today?" he asked.

"Yes, sir," Purna replied.

"Please sit down," he said, and so she did in the chair nearby.

He looked for the keys to the drawer in both the pockets of his coat and, having found them, placed them on the table.

"Did I give you your bill?" he said, frustrated.

"Yes, you did. I have brought the bill and the money." Purna laid both of them on the table and stood up. He took the money and licked his finger to count the notes. He put the money in the drawer and locked it, stamped a receipt, and gave it to Purna.

"Tomorrow we are vacating, so please let the senior doctor know," Purna added.

"Yes, I will," he said without lifting his head.

Malati lay in bed with her eyes closed. Purna put the child to sleep. Malati's heart was tremulous and distressed. Her real place was with Bava, whom she loved. *One day I will meet him. There is only one way for the future. She had to get a job somewhere. I have to raise my son. Mother is suffering. I have to help her in every way.* She interrupted her thoughts when she heard her mother's footsteps and opened her eyes.

"Did you pay all the bills? When are we leaving here?" Malati asked.

"Yes I have paid all the dues; we will leave early morning."

"You are having a lot of trouble, mother," she said sadly.

"How can you not take the trouble?" said Purna disparagingly.

They were both silent for a while.

"The baby does not have any clothes," stated Malati.

"I bought some yesterday," she said and handed the clothes in a paper parcel. Malati took out the clothes and said, "These may be too big."

"These are the only ones available. They do not have smaller than these. He will grow into them." Purna was matter of fact.

She cooked some food meant for new mothers, and

both of them ate. She washed the baby's clothes and hung them out to dry and tidied the room.

The next morning, even before Malati woke up, she mixed two glasses of coffee. She stuffed all the kitchen utensils in a gunny bag and tied it up. By the time Malati woke, all the packing was done.

"Wash your face and drink your coffee. I will go and bring a couple of autos."

"I was thinking all night," said Malati, rubbing her eyes.

Purna, surprised, wondered, *What did she think all night?* She looked at her.

"We will name him Ramamurthy, after Father. I will call him Rambabu," she said.

"Fine," Purna said curtly with some hurt peeping inside her.

"We have to give him all the childhood immunizations, don't we?"

"The doctor told us to go to Niloufer Hospital. We will get it done; first have your coffee," she said and went towards the gate.

Malati washed her face and poured the coffee into a glass from the flask and drank it. In the meantime, Purna returned with the autos. Malati sat in the auto filled with stuff, and Purna sat in the other with a few more belongings and the baby. They reached the rented room.

Malati adjusted to troubles and inconveniences. The room was neither big nor too small. It had good light and ventilation. Purna converted the veranda into a kitchen. Malati realized all the trouble her mother took. *Where was the man, the provider in this household?* Malati agonized. There were only troubles.

She spread a mat, placed the child on it, and sat with him. Deep but formless thoughts engrossed her. *Why did this happen? Why did fate cheat me? Will I ever see Bava? Suppose I could write to him, but he hasn't replied to the ones I wrote.* Her thoughts turned to tears.

Purna, walking between the room and the veranda, noticed Malati's tears. "Lie down for a while on the mat," she said. "You may get dizzy with weakness."

Purna was not touched by tears or thoughts.

She came back to the room and started searching for something in a bag.

"What are you looking for?" asked Malati, who was lying on the cot.

"I don't know where I placed the match box. I don't seem to remember."

"You did not drop them in the bag; you put them in the can," Malati said.

Purna took the matchbox from the can. She managed to cook some rice and brought it to Malati, who ate a few morsels in silence and washed her hands in the plate. Purna also stuffed a few bites and slept on another mat. As soon as she lay down, her head filled with thoughts turning her upside down.

*Today we have settled in this room. I have to transfer the money to Hyderabad from Visag. Subbiah used to take care of all these matters for me. I had a brother to care for me. There is no one to call my own. No one to advise or help me here. With the birth of this new baby, Malati will not be married now. If mine was a lonely life, I never imagined that Malati's also would become a lonely one.*

Thoughts tormented her all night. That Malati was not prudent bothered her. All that should not have happened had happened. Malati would raise the child and spend her whole life doing so and be with him. The fate written on one's forehead cannot be escaped. Husband, marriage, and the pleasures thereof, all these are foreign to Malati now. Thinking of all that had happened, Purna drowned in sorrow.

# Chapter Twenty-eight

A big change came over Bhaskar these days. He was preoccupied and looked as if searching for something he had lost. He looked defeated and severely hurt. Not only his parents but the servants also noticed that he was in a daze. One day Lalita raised the subject of Seshagiri Rao's daughter, and he barked at her. Lalita was reticent after that. *Maybe he loves some girl in the college, and he is hesitating to tell us, as we may not approve*, thought Raja Rao. One day at dinner, he raised the question of marriage.

"I don't want to get married now. There is no need for you to look for alliances," Bhaskar said firmly.

"Why? Are you going to be a bachelor all your life?" Raja Rao said, raising his decibel.

Bhaskar finished his dinner in silence.

"His heart may be with Malati," said Raja Rao to his wife.

"They have left without telling us," said Lalita defiantly.

"It has been more than seven or eight months since they left. They have not even written," he said, surprised. Lalita did not have the courage to answer this question.

Bhaskar was morose and in agony every day. He went to the hospital at eight o'clock and performed his duties and night calls. He attended to all his patients diligently and worked mechanically. Since his mind was not with him, he called the doctors "sister" and vice versa. His friends realized that he was not himself and was withdrawn. This disturbed Lalita. She did not realize the intensity of his love for Malati. She thought he would forget her if she was out of sight. Now she realized her mistake. She wanted to talk to him and ask what bothered him. She would go and sit with him, but then her thoughts scattered and the lips froze. If it was true that Malati was a mother, the very thought made her tremble. There was no redemption.

Raja Rao also was absentminded. He did not talk like he used to. When he did, he weighed his words. He did not take interest in anything, not even in Bhaskar's studies or his work. He did not make any attempts to further Bhaskar's career. He was not even tending the garden. His heart taunted him. Everyone's lives have ups and downs, but in Purna's life, there were only downs and valleys. Raja Rao felt helpless and miserable.

# Chapter Twenty-nine

In the evening at the hospital, patients were eagerly anticipating the arrival of their dear ones. Prameela was in the hospital in a private ward, and hence had permission to have an attendant all twenty-four hours. Ayah Adamma stayed with her when her husband, Shekhar, would go to the high court during the day and visit in the evening. On holidays, he was with her all day. That evening, it was past six thirty. Prameela waited at the door for her husband and son. Every day at six, her husband would be there with Raghu, their five-year-old son. Adamma would go home in the car, have a bath and dinner, and return within an hour. Shekhar would be with his wife until eight o'clock and return home with their five-year-old.

At visiting time, there was a lot of bustle at the hospital, with families of patients arriving in crowds. It was already three months since Prameela was admitted to the hospital. That evening, Shekhar had not yet come. She was peeved. Every day he would give a different excuse for the delay. Even after many reminders, he was not able to come early. Prameela lay restless. The

doctors made not one or two, but innumerable tests.
She had X-rays, more than one. Doctors, not one
but four, had examined her. They discussed among
themselves and gave their consultations. They even
brought a doctor who had received further training
abroad. If she did not get operated on, it would be
life-threatening, but if she did, she had a chance for
a healthy life. This was the consensus. But she was
daunted. "I am fine, so why do I need this operation?"
The doctors decided, and her husband was agreeable.
There was no one for Prameela to confide in, and no
one to hear her. If she survived the operation, fine, but
if she did not? What would happen to her young son?
Good times lay ahead of her. What had she seen and
what had she experienced? Who would take care of
the child if anything happened to her? Shekhar was
not able to handle his own court duties; how would
he take care of the house? If a woman stays home
and takes care of the house, the man can go to work
peacefully. Now that she has been in the hospital for
three months, the house must be in a mess. *Men don't
seem to realize the value of a woman,* she thought. *If she
goes out of town for a day, he gets perturbed. Even though
there are many servants and workers, what is the use?
There is no home without the mistress. Many women have
managed when widowed, but as soon as the wife dies, the
man starts looking for alliances and becomes a bridegroom.*

Prameela contemplatively wove a garland with her
thoughts. Shekhar arrived.

"Finally you have come. What was the delay?
Where is Raghu? Didn't he come?" She showered him
with questions.

"He did not come. He is playing with the children

in the neighborhood. I have told the cook to keep an eye on them. Anyway, Adamma is going home. I will have her bring him with her when she returns," said Shekhar in reply.

"Do you know how long I have been waiting for you?" she said with a pout.

"What can I do, Pramee? No matter how hard I try, I get delayed. I have told you many times, that by the time I come home from court, I have asked them to keep the basket ready, but they always give me some excuse, and it is delayed. The milk has not come yet, or the man who went to buy fruits has not returned," he said, frustrated.

Driver Venkiah brought the basket into the room. He set the food on the table and the clothes in the almira. Adamma took the utensils of the previous day and the dirty clothes in the basket and went home.

"Yes, if I am not home, the servants will not work properly," Prameela said.

"Never mind; we will adjust for a few days."

"How is Raghu?"

"What's with him? He is fine."

"You have to watch him a little; he plays with his food."

"Why watch him? We both eat at the same time. I have him across from me and coax him to eat. You do not have to worry about him. Tell me how you are?"

"You dropped me off here. They say they have to operate. I am afraid. Why do I need this operation?" she appealed to him.

"Everyone is afraid of an operation. Do you know how many operations they perform every day? Why should you be afraid? Tell me."

"I am the one to have the operation, not you! That is why you are so brave," she said angrily

"Pramee, if I could have your illness, I would take it."

"I am sorry. When you are so brave, I reacted. If you are going to be operated on the head, will you not be scared?" She looked him straight in the eye.

"Not scared? I am also scared. There is God above for everything," he said and he turned away to hide his tears.

Prameela softened. Silence filled the room.

"Isn't it the day after tomorrow that the operation is fixed? "

"Yes," he said softly, taking her hand into his.

"You should definitely bring Raghu tomorrow evening; I will look at him to my heart's content," she said in a broken voice.

"The doctor said it is not possible tomorrow. You will be sedated. Adamma will bring him now and I will bring him again in the morning. I have told them that I cannot work for a few days."

"Look," she pleaded.

"What?"

Her eyes were full of tears. "You have to promise one thing."

'What is it?"

"I read Raghu an English story. Do you know what he said on hearing it?"

"The story is nice; read me another."

"You joke at everything."

"No, Pramee, I know what is on your mind."

"He firmly said, 'Mother, I never want a stepmother,'" she said and turned her face away.

Shekhar was losing courage but was able to say, "Don't be crazy. Stay calm."

"No, I am just expressing my feelings. I am scared of this operation. If I am not there, Raghu will definitely pine for me. Your aunt is in town; call her to help. But don't you get married because there is no lady in the house. Promise me." She stretched out her hand. Shekhar placed his hand on hers.

"You will be safe and healthy and will come home. You will take care of me and the child. You will be a mother to him for another hundred years. How can you be so scared? Yesterday they performed this surgery on a five-year-old. He was not scared like you."

"How do you know that he was not scared? Ask him. Ask his parents how many Gods they prayed to. They will tell you."

Meanwhile, Adamma arrived.

"What? Raghu did not come?" she asked, disappointed.

"No, Amma, he is playing at home. 'I won't go with you; I will go with dad,' he said."

"Did you see? Already everyone is forgetting me."

"What are you saying? He is only a child; he was busy playing and did not want to come with Adamma. You don't have to get disheartened."

Prameela did not reply.

"Don't let any crazy ideas come near you I will bring him in the morning." Shekhar patted Prameela on the back.

# Chapter Thirty

ChandraShekhar was an advocate in Hyderabad. He did not have a big practice, but it was not small, either. He made a good living. He had his own house in Khairatabad. His father had bought the land and built a house, and Shekhar improved on it by adding more conveniences. The garden around the house was beautiful. There was only one gate. Both the pillars were lighted. On the right side, a nameplate was hanging with his name written in big letters in both English and Telugu.

When everything was fine, fate did not seem to like it. Prameela fainted one day. She had never fallen sick before. As the doctors wanted her to get admitted, she did so the same day. Tests and investigations were done, and it was determined that she needed to have brain surgery. She had been in the hospital for some months.

Shekhar came home from the hospital.

"Nanna." Raghu came running to the car.

"Why didn't you come to the hospital with Adamma?" he asked affectionately.

Raghu bent his head as if he made a major blunder.
"Never mind. You can come with me tomorrow. We
will go early in the morning."

"I will get ready early in the morning," he said
perkily, having been forgiven.

That night Shekhar could not sleep. Prameela being
disheartened was on his mind. He was also dejected.
He could not allay his own fears, either. What if she
does not come home alive as she said? That thought
shook him. Since the time his wife went to the hospital,
Raghu slept with him. Three days ago, he signed all
the papers the nurse had given and signed the consent
for surgery. *Should I cancel the surgery?* was his thought
today. *Can I live without Prameela? No, I should not get
these negative thoughts. How many people have survived
surgery? How many more have gone home cured? Only
the ones alive are there. But the people who died are not
there. Don't know how many have died.*

Shekhar was tormented with thoughts flooding his
mind and was unable to handle it. *She worried that
I would get a stepmother for Raghu. Silly girl. Mother's
heart will hurt that way. Mother is the child's world and
if that mother is lost?* He looked at the clock. Each
minute felt like an age. That night the minute hand
did not move at all. It seemed to have stopped. Its
heart was still beating; it had not stopped.

The alarm sounded at four thirty in the morning.
He remembered that the surgery was scheduled for
this morning. The calendar hanging on the wall was
driving him crazy. His heart told him that Prameela
did not need the surgery. *I will go to the hospital in
the morning and take back the signed consent, as she is
nervous. Who can escape fate? Whatever is to be will be. I*

*will bring Prameela home. I shall cancel the surgery.*

His legs were dangling loose; he was surprised. *I do not know of any such weakness.* The clock had never moved so slowly. The servants were all snoring. Raghu was sleeping peacefully with a glowing face. He was in the sleep of the innocent, with the radiance of the pure. *I may be unlucky, but he is lucky. He will not lose a mother. Oh, God!*

There are many patients in the hospital, and how many have had operations? How many more are going to have it? A variety of diseases and serious diseases, there is no discrimination between young and old; they are of all ages. They are from all walks of life. Sounds like hell, but it is a heaven. The doctors are God-like. How much they toil for people swimming between life and death. How many thousands of them? The medical profession is very noble. How many people look forward to and wait for the doctor, their words as if quoted from the Vedas. Somewhere the clock struck five. Shekhar looked at the clock in his room, which confirmed that the time indeed was five.

"Venkiah," he shouted. Venkiah, who was sleeping in the hall, woke up with a start. Rubbing his eyes, he came to him, saying, "Babu?"

"Do you know my maternal uncle's house in town?"

"Yes, sir, I do."

"Go there and bring them here in the car. Tell them it is urgent."

"Sure, I will." Venkiah left with long strides.

Shekhar looked at the clock again; it was five thirty. He looked at the gate through the window. The car went past the gate. He looked at Raghu to see if he was awake. *What if Prameela does not come home alive?*

*What is the future of this child?* Tears poured down his face. Awaiting his uncle, he finished his bath and sat in the front room. The car that went at five fifteen came back at six thirty. He went to the door.

"Come in, Uncle," he said and brought him in.

"Why have you sent for me?" his uncle asked.

"Prameela is very sick."

"What, a fever?"

"Yes, it would have been good if it was just a fever."

The uncle was anxious to hear the news. Shekhar motioned to his uncle to sit, and they both sat down.

"One day, Prameela fell unconscious and was so for a few hours. I took her to the hospital. They did a lot of investigations. They say she needs brain surgery."

"What? Brain surgery?" The uncle was startled.

"Yes," said Shekhar softly.

Silence stood between them for a few minutes. The uncle was aghast.

"Is the operation necessary?" he asked, very concerned.

"They said that if they do not operate, it will be more problematic in the future. I don't know what to do."

"What does Prameela say?"

"What can she say? She is very scared."

"Other than the doctors in the hospital, could you not get another opinion?"

"Ten doctors have seen her by now."

"How long is it since she has been in the hospital?"

"She fell unconscious three months ago and was admitted the same day."

"Brain surgery is scary," said the uncle, trembling.

The cook brought some coffee and upma. Shekhar

handed over one plate and placed the coffee glass close to him.

"Nanna, I am ready," said Raghu, running to his father, who held him tightly.

"Do namaskaram to Uncle." Shekhar put the child's hands together, and he turned away shyly.

Shekhar and Uncle had their tiffin and coffee and placed the empty dishes on the table.

"Shall we go now?" asked Shekhar, and the three went to the hospital.

On seeing Raghu, Prameela's face brightened.

"Greetings, Uncle. So you have also come." She stretched out her hands and pulled the child close to her, holding him close to her heart and showering him with kisses on his head, neck, and eyes. On witnessing this maternal bond, both Shekhar and Uncle were moved. Raghu suffocated under his mother's caress.

Motherhood is so intense. When the newborn is thrust into this world, if the love to care for them is not planted in the heart of a mother, who else will care to nourish and protect these young ones? This is all God's creation, and this creation is an illusion.

"Pramee, how are you, dear? Did you sleep well last night?" Shekhar drew a chair close to her and sat down. The uncle sat in a chair a little farther away.

"Uncle, did you see this injustice? I am to have an operation. Do you see any illness in me? It seems I fainted; they did tests and decided to operate. And this gentleman agreed to it," Prameela appealed to her uncle.

"That's true, dear; you don't look sick. You can go home quite happily."

"Uncle, until I come home, why don't you and Aunt

stay with us? If Aunt is at home, then I will not worry so much about the house."

"All right, I shall go and bring her this morning. You don't have to worry about the house. We will take care of Raghu and Shekhar."

"What is there to take care of me?" said Shekhar standing up.

"That is what he says. Every day there is confusion before going to court. Where is my watch? Where is my pen? Every day we are searching for things."

"I am not going to court until you come home."

"There is no better decision than that," said Prameela satisfied.

"You take rest," they said. Shekhar and Uncle got up to leave.

"Where is Raghu?" Prameela looked around.

"Must be in the veranda," replied Shekhar.

"Uncle, please go and bring Aunt," Prameela reminded him.

"Surely," said the uncle.

Uncle and Shekhar came home with grieving faces. In the evening, Aunt, Uncle, and Shekhar went to the hospital. Prameela was sedated and in a deep sleep. She tried to open her eyes, but they were heavy and drooping. She could hear what was being said but could not open her lips to speak. Everyone asked the same question. "How is this going to end?" Shekhar was not able to bear the sight of his wife being semiconscious.

"She seems to be very weak," Shekhar addressed the nurse when she entered.

"Not weakness. She has had an injection," she said as a matter of fact.

The nurse held some papers in her hand. "These

papers are not for this case," she muttered and went to the next room.

The three of them sat in silence for an hour in Prameela's room. They signaled each other with their eyes that they could leave. Shekhar stood at his wife's bedside and stared at her face with wet eyes. She was sleeping. Her eyes were closed. No one could imagine the sorrow in his heart or guess his thoughts. They took a deep sigh and left the room. They reached home with heavy hearts and no one dared start a conversation

"The operation is at eight o'clock tomorrow morning," said Shekhar as he walked into the house.

"We can go there by seven thirty," said the uncle.

"Venkiah, bring the car in the morning at seven."

"We need to fill it with petrol," said Venkiah.

"Then come at six."

"Yes, sir," said Venkiah.

# Chapter Thirty-one

Uncle and Shekhar reached the hospital at seven thirty the next morning. They went straight to Prameela's room. They panicked, as she was not there. She had already been moved to the operating theatre. They sat on a bench outside the theatre. When they saw the doctor entering the OT, they stood up.

"Namaskar," said Shekhar respectfully.

"You have come so early. There will be a long delay," said the doctor.

"It is all right."

The doctor disappeared into the OT.

"Doctor seems confident," said the uncle.

"They are used to it, which is why they are not scared," said Shekhar, sitting on the bench and praying to all the Gods. "Should have checked the horoscope. It was a mistake," he regretted. More than an hour passed, and both were still sitting on the bench.

"There is a canteen nearby. Would you like some coffee?" asked Uncle.

"All right," Shekhar said, and the two got up mechanically and drank some coffee. They sat on the bench for another hour. A nurse came out of the theatre.

"Is the operation over?" Shekhar asked anxiously.

"Yes, she is inside in another room," she said and left holding a tray full of surgical instruments.

"When can we see her?" Shekhar asked the nurse when she returned.

"You can go home and come back in the evening. If the doctor gives permission, you can visit with her," she said and left.

"Let's go," Shekhar signaled to Uncle.

"If it is all right with you," Uncle replied, and they went home.

They came early in the evening, accompanied by Aunt.

Prameela's heart was beating, she was breathing, and all other organs were working, but she was still unconscious. The doctors had done all that they needed to do. Blood and glucose were being administered through rubber tubes. They were also giving her injections.

Shekhar and Uncle stayed in the hotel nearby, eating the food that Aunt sent from home. They were in the hospital for three days. Prameela was alive for three days when the doctors lost the battle.

What is your strength compared to mine? Death mocked them.

*This is the end of your life.* The secret was whispered into Prameela's ears.

On the fourth day after the operation, Prameela slipped out of this world forever.

Shekhar, unable to contain his sorrow, sobbed like a baby. *What should not have happened has happened.*

*Destiny! Why are you testing me like this?* He was shattered. *What Prameela expected has happened. She was afraid. What is the use of medicinal leaves after the hands are burned? Can you be scared of flames after lighting a fire? I should have cancelled the operation. Without the surgery she could have lived some time more without harm.* These thoughts were turning in Shekhar's head. He pushed aside all his thoughts but one now: *Can Raghu see his mother's corpse? Can he bear it? What if he does not see? He is not even six. What would he remember even after viewing? After a few days, he will ask, 'Where is mother? When will she come home from the hospital? How do I answer him? If we take the dead body home, he will definitely see it. Should we send him away to the neighbor's house? No, let him see his mother for the last time.*

He arrived at this decision after much deliberation.

They brought the body home. Shekhar took the child to his room, sat him on his lap, and gave him a big hug.

"Babu," he said, but could not proceed further.

"What?" Raghu's eyes filled with fear as he looked at the father who had tears in his eyes.

"Nanna, you are crying!"

"Mother has left us and gone," Shekhar said in a hoarse voice.

"Where to?" the child asked unhesitatingly.

"To God."

"What will God do with her?"

"Come, child," he said, and holding his hand, he took him to the front hall.

Prameela's body was laid over a white sheet, the head bandage still in place. Aunt had decorated her with turmeric and saffron powder. She draped a flower garland around her, decorated her feet with turmeric. Shekhar stood there petrified and tightly held the child, whose heart was beating rapidly.

A lot of people had gathered: the neighbors, people they knew, and those they did not know. Shekhar had the traditional bath, while Uncle held Raghu close to him and performed all the rituals according to the scriptures. Shekhar was blurry-eyed throughout.

# Chapter Thirty-two

Shekhar had no family without Prameela. Days dragged one by one. Neighbors, friends in town, and relatives from out of town arrived to comfort him. Shekhar was inconsolable, even though he was aware that life and death are inevitable. He tried to be brave for Raghu. If he melted, what would happen to the child? People were sympathetic in different ways, with opinions, suggestions, and philosophy.

"Pangs of separation should not come at this young age," said one close relative.

"The lonely life is unbearable, dear. When my wife died young, I was unable to forget her. Unable to bear the loneliness, I married again within a month," expressed one older man.

"This is what you will say now, when newly bereaved. It is better to marry now when you are young, rather than be in the hands of a daughter-in-law in your last days. You will be trampled," was the opinion of another experienced man.

"It is not a home, if there is no woman in it."

"Someone has to care for the child."

"A house without a woman is not a home, and a home without a woman is the wilderness," said an educated man.

"Poor thing, a stepmother at this young age," said a female voice.

"What if it is a stepmother? A mother has maternal love. A stepmother has the love of nurturing," said an old man's second wife.

"Maternal love will last until she has a child of her own. Then this child's life will be difficult," said a wise one.

Everyone poured out opinions like water, whether they were heard or not. *Each opinion according to individual experience,* thought Shekhar. Immersed in his sorrow, he did not care for opinions nor take them to heart.

After a while, everyone withdrew, even Aunt and Uncle.

All that was left for him were Raghu and a full-sized color portrait of Prameela.

# Chapter Thirty-three

"Saroo, why are you off mood?" asked Sarojini's father, Srihari Rao.

"Nothing, Nanna, I am fine."

"No, child, there is some trouble and sadness on your face, which you are trying to hide. Please tell me."

"Nanna, I am in love with someone," she said shyly.

"Who is that lucky guy?"

"Don't raise hopes in me, Nanna. What if he does not love me?"

"Why won't he? If it is not him, I will get you a good alliance and get you married."

"It is not that. Don't you want to first find out if the one I love returns my love?"

"Who is he?" the father asked lovingly.

"It is Bhaskar. He studied MBBS with me. He got many prizes, too. He endeared everyone to him with his intelligence. It is not just me; everyone respects and admires him."

"I will make enquiries."

Sarojini was pleased.

Srihari Rao, an engineer, had signed many contracts

and earned a lot of money and still was earning. He believed that in this world all things could be achieved with money. "Everything has to bow to money," he said. He was ignorant in his arrogance. He was able to succeed in life with this strong belief. His daughter was in love with Bhaskar. Just as he could buy cigarettes and matches in the paan shop with money, he thought that he would pocket Bhaskar for his daughter. He laughed with contempt. He acted as if the marriage between Bhaskar and his daughter was a done deal. He did not think that there would be a problem. Srihari Rao wondered how to start the quest.

"Saroo, we will have a big party for your birthday."

"What, Nanna? My birthday is over," she said, surprised.

"What if it is over? We will have another birthday," he said, smiling.

Sarojini laughed. "Nanna! You do get unusual ideas."

"'Those with no imagination should not stay in town,' is the saying. Life is a garland of problems. To solve those problems, one needs imagination." Srihari Rao was smug.

"Nanna!" Sarojini was filled with happiness and gave him a big hug.

"Say it is your birthday, and invite all your friends. Tell Bhaskar to definitely come. I will not let that opportunity pass by. I will talk to him."

Once the birthday bash was decided, arrangements were being made with all pomp and splendor. The canopy was set up in Srihari Rao's house. The birthday celebrations were more like that of a wedding. The invitations were printed. There was hustle and bustle in the house for a week. Sarojini handed out the invitations personally by visiting each person, as the invitation was in her name. The invitees concluded that it would be an announcement of an engagement and congratulated her for the same.

"It's not that," she said coyly.

We won't believe it," said a friend.

"Why are you so shy, even though you are a doctor?"

"Oh, she will have her father proudly make the announcement," said another.

She went to Bhaskar with the invitation. He was busy writing.

"Bhaskar," she called out softly. He raised his head.

"I hope I did not disturb you when you are so industrious."

"Oh, no, that's nothing. You have some invitation in hand."

"This Sunday we are having a party at our home; you must definitely attend."

"Sure, I will try."

"Not try, you must definitely come."

"You can see in this hospital how people come with major illnesses and get well. Some come with a minor problem and die. We can dream, but all we desire does not happen. We plan, but it slips away from our hands, so how can I tell you that I will definitely come? Trying is the only one in our hands. What do you say?"

Sarojini was taken aback.

"Bhaskar, you seem to have had a major tragedy in life, or else why would you have this attitude when young and approaching life?" She was pained.

"Tragedy does not have to come to us; we can see other people's tragedies and be affected."

"If I keep talking to you, I will also become an ascetic."

"That's why you should leave me alone."

"How can anyone leave you alone? Instead of me taking to your ways, you could change to our ways. Life is not always sorrow. There is much sweetness, also. You must come to the party," she said and looked intensely into his eyes.

"Sure, I will try my level best."

The long-awaited birthday came. The house shone with decorations of mango leaves and the white *rangoli* at the entrance. All the trees were lighted with garlands of multicolored bulbs. Lights and streamers decorated the walls. Colored streamers were also hanging from the ceiling, and the house was decorated in every way possible.

The servants were wearing new clothes. Sarojini wore her mother's diamonds, which were shining brilliantly. Srihari Rao, standing aloof, looked impatient, surmising; if anyone would assess those diamonds, they could guess how much taxes were evaded. He was nervous. *But they will also know how lucky and rich she is,* he thought, looking around him with pride. His wife, Meena, was also heavily laden with jewelry and unable to walk at a normal pace. He noticed that, too.

"Why don't you sit for a while," he said, frustrated.

As if waiting for instructions, Meena sat down on the sofa nearby. The time had come for the guests to arrive, but Sarojini had not come down yet. Srihari sent the maid Ratnamma to call her, who met her as she was descending the stairs. She looked so beautiful and perfect that her parents were mesmerized. Her father looked at her with joy.

"How is my hairdo?" said Sarojini, bending her head a little.

"It is like Sage Valmiki's," her father said.

"What, Nanna, always joking. Amma, tell me, how is my hairdo?"

"You look good," she said, pleased.

They were waiting for the guests. Srihari Rao and his wife were at the entrance. The servants were at attention. Colorful gourmet dishes decorated the many tables that were placed around the garden. Guests arrived one by one. They were shaking hands with Srihari Rao, and some joined their hands together in greeting. As all of them were Sarojini's friends, she introduced each one by name to her father and then took them to where her mother was sitting. Everyone who was invited arrived except a couple who had sent their regrets that morning. All of them brought gifts. Bhaskar had not come yet. Sarojini, restless, would go to the entrance looking for him. She was ecstatic when she heard the sound of a scooter. Bhaskar had arrived, and she beamed.

"This is Dr. Bhaskar," she said to her father respectfully.

Her mother got up and joined them. "This is my mother."

Bhaskar greeted Meena, who looked him up and down and studied him.

"We are very happy that you came," said Srihari Rao, jubilant.

"When you didn't come for a long time, I was afraid that you would not," pouted Sarojini.

"Why afraid?" he laughed.

Sarojini was delighted and content. People gathered

at the table at the far end of the garden that had a huge, fancily decorated birthday cake. There were twenty-two candles on it. Having blown them out in three puffs, Sarojini cut the cake to applause. She gave the first piece to Bhaskar.

"I will take it after the others," he said, declining. Sarojini was hurt.

"He is inauspicious at every point." She was sick at heart.

Srihari Rao looked at Bhaskar without blinking. Wherever he moved, Srihari Rao followed.

*Handsome boy. Passed all his exams with prizes. Has money. We will be lucky to have him as a son-in-law.*

His wife thought the same. One server gave Meena a plate filled with food.

*Those who have money are lucky, and those who are lucky have everything,* thought Srihari Rao.

Sarojini was attentive to Bhaskar at every opportunity; she was glued to him. People were walking around with plates and cups filled with food and drink. Some lay down empty cups on the table, and some placed them under the main table. The servers were handing out ice cream in small cups with spoons. Some said "yes," and some others declined. Her parents were thrilled at Sarojini mixing with the guests, but followed Bhaskar all the time. The party was in keeping with his status, riches, and rank. Srihari Rao was satisfied and let out a deep sigh. His wife, Meena, watched Bhaskar and Sarojini without a wink. The guests went to Meena with folded hands and shook hands with Srihari Rao to bid farewell. Gradually, they left one by one. Bhaskar did the same.

"What, you are leaving?" Srihari Rao asked.

"Yes, I have to go. My father is not in town, and my mother is alone and waiting for me."

"Oh, dear, we should have invited her, also. It was an oversight," he said in regret.

Sarojini joined them.

"Goodbye," he said. Sarojini did not stop him, as she felt that he was determined to leave. Bhaskar left.

Srihari Rao was reflective. *It is not going to be easy to pocket Bhaskar. That anyone would fall for the cling of money is false.* All the guests had gone and the three sunk into their sofas.

"The food was good. Where did you get it catered from?" Meena asked, bubbling.

"What does it matter which hotel? The party was a success," said Srihari Rao smugly.

"No one took the *paan*; it all got left over," said Meena.

"Nanna, isn't Bhaskar nice?" said Sarojini to her father.

"He is good but looks a little stubborn."

"Because he is stubborn, he was able to pass all his exams brilliantly."

"But our concern is not in passing exams," said Srihari Rao.

# Chapter Thirty-four

Raghu wandered around lost and fussy, especially at the dining table. He was troublesome. Unable to express his sorrow, he cried for no obvious reason. Everyone felt sorry for him, as this was the age to sit on a mother's lap and be naughty. Fate had separated the bud at the time of bloom.

Shekhar held him on his lap and coaxed him to eat and also had the child sleep with him. He gave up his other activities and spent all his time with his son. He made every attempt that the child's heart know no sorrow. But the young heart searched for his mother. The little heart was edgy. Shekhar, an adult, was unable to handle the separation, so what of this young child? Raghu would call out to his mother for everything. *Now he says 'Amma,' and then corrects it to 'Nanna.' Dear God! Are these your pranks? What pleasure do you get out of all this? What satisfaction? Separating a child from its mother. Separating a loving couple. Is this fair?* Taunted by his thoughts, tears overflowed on to his face.

One night after dinner, as they were lying in bed, Raghu asked Shekhar, "Do you have a mother?"

Shekhar was surprised. Whatever was the child thinking?

"No, dear, I don't have a mother," he said slowly. Raghu then got out of his bed and came to his father.

"Nanna, as you are crying, I have come near you."

Shekhar took the child close to him.

"Nanna."

"Yes, dear."

"Can I ask you something?"

"Ask, child, whatever you want, ask."

"I don't want anything."

"Tell me, child. What is it you want?"

"Adamma said—" He stopped.

"What did she say?"

"You said, 'God took mother away.' How did she go there?"

"What can I say?"

"Adamma said that Mother died. And those who die are burned." He hid his face in the pillow.

"True, if they are burned, then they can go to God."

"Can I ask you another?"

"Ask, Raghu, there is no need to be afraid of me." He held him close.

Raghu hesitated to ask.

"Why are you quiet? Ask."

"Shall I ask?"

"Ask," the father cajoled.

"How far have you studied?"

"Why? Did I do something wrong?"

"No, whenever I ask Adamma a question, she says, 'I am not educated. Ask your father.'"

"Is that all?"

"Nanna, does God know only Hindi and not know

any other language?"

"Why not? God knows all languages."

"But I am not educated at all."

"Shall I read you a story?"

"I have to write a letter."

"To whom?"

"God."

"To God?" the father paled. "What do you want to write? I will write it."

Raghu got a sheet of white paper and a pencil from the desk.

Shekhar's eyes were moist. "Raghu, shall I get you another mother?"

"Oh, no! I am afraid of these women," he said and sat on the bed. "Write the letter," he ordered.

"What should I write?" the father asked sadly.

"Raghu wants a mother. What will you do with my mother? Everyone has a mother. Me and Nanna do not have a mother. So please send mother back quickly."

"Is that it?" said Shekhar, pained.

"That's all." He jumped from the bed, snatched the letter from his father, and ran.

"Child! What are you going to do with the letter?"

"I will burn it. It will go to God."

"Adamma! He wants to burn the letter. Be careful," yelled Shekhar.

Shekhar did not know what to do. It was over two months since he went to work. *Can I leave Raghu in this condition? How do I solve this?*

"Nanna, I burned the letter," Raghu said as he came back into the room.

Shekhar sat him on his lap. "I will send you to

school. Will you go?"

"What will be there?"

"There will be children like you, and you can play with them. They will also teach you."

"All right, I'll go," Raghu said cheerfully.

"Then go to sleep. In the morning, we will go to school."

Raghu woke up early the next morning, enthused to go to school. Shekhar and Raghu got ready and came to the dining table for breakfast. Shekhar coaxed him to eat. He drank his milk. They left about eight thirty. The driver stopped the car and opened the door for them to alight. The cheer that was at home waned, and Raghu looked scared. Shekhar noticed that the child was nervous. The school building had long verandas surrounded by a beautiful garden. The site and environment were pleasant. They got down from the car. The school's peon came towards them and asked them what they wanted. Shekhar told him that he wished to admit the child. The peon looked at Raghu distastefully and went in. He brought back a piece of paper and a pencil and said to "write purpose of visit and name." Raghu was apprehensive.

Shekhar wrote the necessary details. They were led to the principal's office. He was at his desk, looking through some files. Shekhar approached him and said, "Namaskaram." Raghu hid behind his father. The principal motioned to him, and Shekhar and Raghu sat opposite him.

"What is your name?" asked the principal, addressing Raghu, who bent his head shyly. "Raghu," he said softly without raising his head.

"Raghu means Raghu Kumar, Raghu Ram, or

what?" said the principal, smiling.

"Raghupati," replied Shekhar.

"Raghupati is a nice name. Will you come to our school?"

Raghu shook his head to mean, "No."

"The school admissions are over. You should have come a week or two ago," said the principal regretfully.

"I did not plan on sending him to school. My wife died two months ago."

"Your wife means mother," whispered Raghu in his father's ear.

"Yes, dear, wait awhile. Let me talk to him."

"Since my wife died, he has been fearful. I thought that if he joins the school, he will be playing with other children."

"You are in a bad situation, but I will take you as a special case," said the principal sympathetically.

He removed an application from a pile of papers and gave them to Shekhar.

"Many thanks," Shekhar said and filled out the forms with all the details and his signature.

"How much do I pay?" Shekhar asked.

"You don't have to pay now; we will send you the invoice. Come with me; I shall show you his classroom." The principal got up. The three went to the classroom.

Raghu was nervous the first day, but he got used to the school. The first few days he would not talk to anyone, but gradually he started liking school, which was a big relief to Shekhar. He decided to get back to work and informed his clerk Ramayya.

Shekhar's two juniors had taken care of matters for him during his absence. Some cases had gone to trial; some other clients withdrew and sought other lawyers.

Shekhar was pleased that Raghu liked the school, and this gave him some peace.

Prameela frequently entered his heart. Thoughts of the hospital, the operation, and the funeral gave him the shivers. Silly girl made me promise. She was scared that I would bring a stepmother for Raghu. She thinks men have no heart. But that's the way of the world, which is why she was suspicious. For whatever reason, a man cannot live without a wife. All those who came to console him were of the same opinion. Relatives and friends all suggested remarriage. In this great land of Bharat was born the great Rama—He the one—the believer of one wife for a lifetime.

He went to work the next day.

# Chapter Thirty-five

"Someone named Srihari Rao, an engineer, has come in a car and gave this card." The servant handed over a white visiting card to Raja Rao, who was in the hall reading the newspaper.

"Where is he?" asked Raja Rao, turning the card over.

"They parked the car at the gate."

"Ask them to come in." Raja Rao went inside. The car drove in.

Srihari Rao walked in and sat down on the sofa. The servant turned on the ceiling fan. He looked around the four corners and appreciated the house, but it was old. It must be an ancestral home, but not as attractive as his.

Raja Rao walked in, having changed his clothes.

"Namaskaram," said Raja Rao, greeting him with folded hands.

"Namaskaram," said Srihari Rao, standing up. "I came without informing you; I hope you are not busy with other matters," he apologized.

"Oh, that's nothing. Sit down." Both seated

themselves.

"I am an engineer in this town."

"Is that so? I am glad to hear that."

"All the big houses in this area have been raised by my hands," Srihari Rao said with pride.

"Are yours independent contracts?"

"Other companies, I cannot work for. People have to work under me. I will never work for anyone at any time," he bragged.

"When you have work in hand and luck favors you, there is no need to work for anyone else."

"Well said," Srihari Rao smirked. The cook brought coffee in glasses and biscuits on a plate.

"Why all this, now?" said Srihari Rao, picking up the coffee.

"This is nothing much," Raja Rao replied.

"The main reason that I have come here is—I won't waste your time too much—is to request you …" He settled into the sofa. "My daughter and your son studied in the same college. My daughter also graduated from medical school this year."

"I am very happy."

"We want to get her married. Your son attended my daughter's birthday party. I request that you, your wife, and son visit us at our house." He expressed his wishes very clearly.

"I will check with my son."

"The telephone number is on my card. You can call me and come at your convenience." Srihari Rao rose to leave.

They both exchanged namaskars in the veranda. As soon as Srihari Rao left, Lalita came out excitedly, as she was eavesdropping from inside.

"Srihari Rao's wife comes to our club. What shiny diamonds. She does not repeat her jewelry or her sarees. They are very rich."

"He wants his daughter to marry your son."

"Our boy is sitting on the mountain. No girl is good enough. He gets peevish, and if I persist, he gets angry."

"That peevishness and anger comes from you."

"You don't miss any opportunity to criticize me."

"Let's reply to them within a week. If we are not marrying her, at least they can look elsewhere. The girl knows him. I believe Bhaskar attended a party at their home."

"Where he goes or where he wanders, he does not inform me. His life is spent on the scooter. Whatever, we should not miss this alliance. This is their only daughter. They don't have anyone before or after her."

"If we do not want to miss this alliance, then convince him. Whoever he likes and agrees to is fine," Raja Rao said sternly.

"I will tell him very strongly. We'll see."

Lalita eagerly awaited Bhaskar's return. This alliance should not be missed. Bhaskar reached home at eight thirty. As usual, on his arrival, they sat down for dinner. There was silence for a while.

"Bhaskar." Raja Rao started the conversation. "Today Srihari Rao came. You went to their house for a party, I believe."

"Yes, why?"

"Their daughter studied with you, I believe."

"Yes."

"They wanted us to visit them once."

"What for?"

"What for? A daughter of marriageable age and a son of marriageable age," said Lalita enthusiastically.

Bhaskar had heard those words before under different circumstances, but the words were the same. He was pained. On seeing the hurt on his face, the parents discontinued the matter.

"I will write to them that you are not interested in marriage at this time," said Raja Rao and ended the matter.

"Please do," said Bhaskar curtly.

Lalita's dreams were extinguished.

# Chapter Thirty-six

Purna, Malati, and little Rambabu had been in the one-room apartment for over four years now. In that place, Rambabu took his first steps, and both Purna and Malati were overjoyed. Now at four, he was very naughty. Purna was finding it difficult as expenses were increasing, but she did not express this aloud. Malati, however, was cognizant that her mother was struggling for money. Rambabu wanted to buy everything that he saw. Money was not enough. Nowadays the mother was skipping meals. She also skipped drinking coffee.

One day Malati told her mother, "Rambabu is getting big. There is no need for me to be at home. I will look for a job."

Purna heard from Malati what she wanted to say.

"True. It is good to try at any place. But these days, what kind of a job will a school final pass get?"

Malati was dejected.

"I will type somewhere. I need a certificate even for that. No office will take me. I will try privately, even for a lesser salary," she said blandly.

Malati started job hunting. She entered doors and

walked out of them. She was trying for even a petty job. There was no vacancy anywhere. Some places where there were vacancies did not hire girls. "Why do you need a job, lady?" "You should get happily married and run a house," suggested others.

But still she struggled—meandered, walked, went by bus. She was humbled to ask just for a small job. To feed one's hunger, how many people have been struggling and trying in this country? Malati did not give up her attempts. How could she stop? This is life. This is the world. You wake up in the morning hungry. If there was no hunger, the world would be a different place. To suppress this hunger, you need money. If one took to stealing or to fraudulent means, it was to satisfy this hunger.

She was not able to give Rambabu nutritious food. At night her mother was giving him water instead of milk. Malati noticed this but was unable to say anything. Every time she thought about the child being deprived of food, Malati was in agony.

She was riding the bus all day in search of a job. One day she was in Chikkadpally, and another day she was at Malakpet. She had scoured the twin cities, but nowhere could she find even a small job. No one was encouraging. They looked at her vilely. Some replied politely, and many others were rude. One day, when she was going in the bus along Khairatabad Road, she saw a board in English and Telugu at Shekhar's gate. She got down and went in. There was no sign to say, "Beware of dog." She entered the gate and pressed the switch next to a bell-shaped picture. A servant opened the door.

"Who do you want?" he growled.

"Is the lady home?" she asked, placating.

"Madam, you have come here by mistake."

"Isn't this advocate Shekhar's house?"

"Yes."

"Is the master at home?"

"Yes, he is."

"I want to meet him."

"Regarding what matter?"

"I will tell him about my matter."

"Narasimhulu, who is there?" shouted Shekhar from inside.

"Some lady has come."

"Ask her to sit down. I am coming."

Malati sat down, looking around her. Shekhar came out of his office room. Malati stood up.

"Sit down," Shekhar said politely and sat across her. "What brings you here?" he asked her gently.

"We are in a very poor state, my mother, my child, and me. Each day is very difficult. We are living in one room and even paying the rent—"

Even before she could finish, he asked without hesitation, "Where is your husband working?"

"I don't have a husband," she said, bending her head and shrinking into herself.

Not having got over the loss of his wife, Shekhar acutely appreciated her loss. Silence hovered over them. *Bring your aunt over to take care of the child*, he remembered Prameela's words. Could the aunt stay here under these circumstances? Her ways were different. She had a large family and her own problems. Would she leave all that and come here for Raghu's sake?

"What kind of work can you do?" he asked softly.

"I passed the school final; I can type."

"Can you take shorthand?"

"No."

"Have you worked anywhere before?"

"No."

"All right, behind this house there is a small room. You can live there. You can type the papers that the office clerk gives you. The salary, I will figure out later," he said and got up.

Malati bowed to touch his feet.

"Oh, don't," he said and lifted her up.

Shekhar was in tears. Any small incident would bring them on.

"Narasimhulu!" he yelled. He came and stood in front of Shekhar.

"Clean up the room at the back. This evening, this lady will be coming." He went into his office. Narasimhulu looked at Malati curiously and left. Malati went home satisfied.

"Mother, I found a job," she said enthusiastically.

"Where?" she said, narrowing her eyes.

"In an advocate's office. The office is at home. It is very far from here. I went by bus."

"Can you go there every day from here, by bus?"

"Let me finish. When the bus stopped at the house, I thought, *Let me enquire*, and I went in. He seems a very large-hearted man. I told him our plight and said that I would do any kind of work. I told him that I could type. I was afraid that he would ask if I had a certificate. He didn't. He said that there was a room at the back of the house and that we could live there."

"What is the pay?"

"He said he would deal with that later. He seems a

nice man. We can move this evening."

'I don't know how many more troubles God has written for us," Purna said.

"When I was not here, did this boy trouble you and cry for me?" Malati asked.

"He didn't cry; he laughed."

"Oh mother, you are always—" She kissed the child.

"We are not in good times; that is why I am afraid of everything. We'll go to that house and see. If we don't like the place, we can always move out. We have no choice. What else is there to do? We have become nomads," she said, feeling low.

The next day, they packed up and went to Shekhar's bungalow. They settled in two autos with their luggage. They searched for the house and found it. They stopped the autos at the gate. The drivers helped them unload. When they arrived, Shekhar and Raghu were not at home. The servants, Adamma and Narasimhulu, looked at them as if they were wild animals.

The room was very clean but small. Purna was happy that she did not have to pay any rent. The bathroom had to be shared with the other servants. Purna found this difficult, but there was no other choice. *One gets used to comforts and troubles*, she thought as she gathered up courage.

The next day at nine, Malati entered the room adjacent to the front veranda. Two juniors were already there, as was Ramayya, the clerk, who was over sixty. The room was quite big. The walls could not be seen, as they were lined with steel shelves full of huge books. Above them were bundles of files of retired cases. Entering the room full of books and surrounded by them, Malati felt as if she was entering Ali Baba's cave. The vast amount of knowledge in all these books bamboozled her. Shekhar had not come to the office yet. Wondering who she was, the three of them stared at her. Ramayya came forward and asked her, "What is it you want, dear?" He was swallowing up her beauty.

"I have been appointed to do some typing work here," Malati replied.

"The boss did not tell me anything about this." Shekhar walked in even before he could finish the sentence.

"Ramayya garu."

"Sir."

"The workload is increasing in our office, and since you cannot handle it all alone, I have—what's your name, Amma?" He looked at Malati.

"Malati."

*Not Malati, but Malli, the delicate jasmine flower,* thought Ramayya.

"From today she will be working in our office," said Shekhar, as if passing an order.

"Can you type?" Ramayya asked sarcastically.

"Yes," Malati replied boldly.

"I will give you the papers that we need for tomorrow. You can type them."

"Sure."

"You sit there in the veranda. I will call you." Ramayya was bossy.

Shekhar was sitting at the big desk with Ramayya handing him some files and large papers. The junior advocates took out some books from the shelves and were reading. They handed some to Shekhar. Venkiah brought the car in a few minutes. Everyone got into the car.

Ramayya looked at Malati and said, "Come tomorrow." He also left in the car to go to court.

Malati went home.

"Why are you back so soon?" asked Purna.

"They have all gone to court. I will go to the bazaar. Did you need anything?"

"There are plenty of things that I need, but I will manage till the end of the month."

Malati went to the bazaar. Purna bathed her grandchild and dressed him.

Adamma, who was sitting across, watched Purna tending her grandson.

"Purnamma garu." Purna turned around.

"Only the three of you have come. Is your son-in-law not in town?" she sneered.

Purna's heart sank when this question came upon her suddenly.

"I don't know when he will come," mumbled Purna.

Adamma got up and left. *That means there is a son-in-law somewhere.* But I had only half an answer, she thought. *I have to tell Ramayya and Narasimhulu in the office that Malati has a husband somewhere.*

Ever since Malati and Purna arrived, the mutterings increased in the office and at home. Purna was unhappy. If Malati knew about this, she would say "Let's get out of here." But to where? This question will follow us wherever we go. Malati returned from the bazaar with a lot of packets. Purna could not keep quiet and divulged Adamma's question. Malati was angry. "Why do they care about my husband?" she said indignantly.

"Why? That is the way of the world. There are two women without a man's protection. And there is a child. If we had given him away to the orphanage that day—"

"Amma, don't say that again." Malati pounced on her.

# Chapter Thirty-seven

The next morning Malati went to the office. She carefully typed the papers that Ramayya had given her. He was very eager to know how much salary she would be getting.

"Sir," he said, approaching Shekhar.

"Yes?" Shekhar said without lifting his head, looking over some papers.

"We have to write accounts. How much should I write as salary for the new typist?"

"Three hundred," said Shekhar with ease.

Ramayya was surprised. *Three hundred! I have been here for so long, and I get three hundred. Malatamma came yesterday, and she gets three hundred! This is unfair.* Ramayya was unhappy at this injustice. *I suppose beauty has a value,* he thought.

# Chapter Thirty-eight

To admit her son into a local school, Malati took leave from the office one day. Rambabu wanted to go to school with Raghu and was throwing a tantrum. Shekhar told her that Rambabu could join Raghu's school. Malati could not afford the higher tuition. Was Shekhar going to pay for the tuition? If so, what would be her status and reputation? Malati was in a quandary but did not want to contradict Shekhar. That day, when Shekhar took Raghu to school, he picked up Rambabu and had him admitted. That evening, on returning from court, he took both the boys to the bazaar. He bought clothes and other necessities required for school. Rambabu, delighted, brought all this to the room. Purna and Malati looked at each other and were surprised. The little one was ecstatic.

# Chapter Thirty-nine

It had been exactly two years since Prameela died. Shekhar would not go anywhere other than to court. He received invitations for feasts and parties, but he did not feel like attending them. He was used to having Raghu by his side for dinner. He did not want to leave him alone. His friends commented, "How long will you be doing this?" They were entreating and encouraging him to move on. They thought if he spent some time at the club that he would get more spirited. When his best friend was going abroad, his friends arranged a fancy dinner at the club. They insisted that Shekhar attend. Shekhar reluctantly agreed and decided to tell Raghu about it. Having noticed his father changing clothes, Raghu came running to him and asked, "Nanna, where are we going?"

"Raghu, I am going to the club tonight. I will have my dinner there, so will you have your dinner at home without fussing?" he asked affectionately.

"I will come with you."

"I cannot take you; I will come back soon."

"Then I will eat after you come back."

"What if I am late?"

"Then I will eat late."

"That's not the way." He shouted for Adamma.

"Sir," she said as she entered.

"Tell him stories and make him eat and let him go to bed early."

"Yes, sir."

"There are no buttons on his shirt. Put some different clothes on him rather than these faded ones."

"These have become small for him; these are what his mother had stitched."

"What? I have been bringing clothes every time I go to the bazaar," he said, dismayed.

"Father, Ramu is wearing them all," said Raghu.

"Is he?" said Shekhar a little louder.

"We told you that they are all small for Raghu," Adamma added.

"If they are small, why did not you tell me?"

"We did not bother you with petty matters."

"Anything concerning Raghu is not a petty matter. Nothing is trivial. Tell me everything concerning Raghu."

"Yes, sir."

Shekhar went to the country club; Raghu was in tears and stood in the veranda until the car was out of sight.

"Come in and eat your food," said Adamma roughly.

"I won't come until father comes home. I will sit right here."

"Have you seen Ramu wearing your clothes?" Adamma glared at him. "Now you won't eat! Your back should get a little heated," she said and gave him two whacks.

Raghu got up crying, "No, Adamma, don't beat me," and he ran from Adamma, who was chasing him.

"I will eat my food; don't beat me."

"That's the way. Get in line," she said, and she lifted him by his arms and plopped him at the dining table and dished out the food.

"This rice is burned," he said, sobbing.

"Eat it. If not, get up and go."

On hearing Raghu's cries, Malati came into the room.

"Why did you beat him?" asked Malati angrily.

"Amma!" Raghu ran to Malati.

"You may go; I can manage him." Adamma was miffed.

"Adamma, he is a motherless child. If you beat him, you are committing a sin."

"Why? You have in your house a fatherless child."

Malati was stunned.

Shekhar was halfway to the club, but his heart was with Raghu.

"Venkiah, turn around. Let's go home," he said.

He was glad that he returned home.

On seeing his father, Raghu went running to him. Malati went home. Adamma was surprised.

Shekhar took Raghu to the dining table and sat him down and looked at the burned rice on the plate.

Adamma did not speak. She was trembling.

Shekhar went into the kitchen and removed the lid over the rice dish.

"When there is plenty of warm rice in this container, why did you have to give him burned food?" he roared.

"I did not see this container," Adamma said nervously.

He lifted the lid from another container.

"There are plenty of curds in this, and you gave him buttermilk?"

"Little master asks for buttermilk."

"Hey, Raghu, did you not want any curds?"

Raghu looked towards Adamma, and she threatened him with her eyes.

"No, I did not want the curds."

Shekhar sat with the child and spoon-fed him. He also had his dinner.

He put Raghu to sleep, but he could not sleep all night. He was very much troubled. That day, Shekhar realized what the situation would be. If he was not at home, Raghu was getting squashed in Adamma's hands. He did not know which way to turn. He was miserable and rolled in bed, helpless and disheartened. There was no other choice.

But when he returned from the club, he noticed that Malati had taken Raghu close to her and consoled him. Raghu and Rambabu were going to school together and playing together. Shekhar felt a little encouraged by this. Whenever possible, he would take both the boys in the car and buy toys, books, and clothes. He would feed them together, tell them stories, and chat with both of them.

# Chapter Forty

One evening, Shekhar came home from the courthouse at six.

"This arrived in the afternoon's post." Narasimhulu handed him the mail. He opened the letter, which informed him that his aunt was coming the next morning. The letter was written by her son, informing that his mother had desired to visit since Prameela's demise, but was unable to visit earlier due to her own ill health. Could he please send someone to the station to receive her? Shekhar read the letter and left it on the table. The cook brought the coffee. Narasimhulu also stood there.

"Narasimhulu, tell driver Venkiah that he has to go to the station in the morning at six. Ask him to check if he needs any petrol."

"Yes, sir," he said and left.

As usual, Shekhar had his dinner with Raghu and Rambabu.

"I am going to the station tomorrow. As the children have holidays, I will take them also. Tell Rambabu's mother to send him here at six in the morning."

The children were jumping with joy.

He can take his son, but why Rambabu? He is getting used to these joy rides in the car, thought Adamma.

The next morning, both the kids went to the station with Shekhar. The train was running late, and the children were running around the railway platform. Shekhar drew both the kids nearer to him when the train was approaching. The coolies stood up in readiness. The train puffed into the station with pride, as if it had reached its unattainable goal. It came to a stop with a hoot. Shekhar was looking into every compartment for his maternal aunt, Krishnaveni, with the two children running after him. She alighted and was looking for whosoever would be receiving her. She saw Shekhar.

"You came yourself? You could have sent one of the servants. She then introduced him to the girl standing behind her. "This is our Chalapati's daughter, Prabha, the third one. As I did not want to travel alone, he sent her along. You have only one son. Who is the other?" she said pointing at Rambabu.

"He and his mother live in the room behind the house," said Shekhar.

"This is not what should happen to you at this young age. When God withdraws his favors, there is nothing we can do." She looked mournful.

"Is this all the luggage you have?" Shekhar said, pointing to the luggage on the platform.

"One box, one bedding, one basket, one flask," she said.

"The flask is in my hands, Grandma," said Prabha.

Shekhar had the coolie pick up the luggage,

and the driver loaded them into the car. Until they reached home, Krishnaveni was philosophizing about loneliness. The kids were tickling each other and being naughty. Aunt could not bear this noise and was simpering now and again. Prabha was quiet.

They reached home. As they entered, they noticed the life-size photo of Prameela in color. This broke Krishnaveni's heart, and she let out a torrent of tears.

"If people like us fall ill, we will be moaning but still be active. Why should she complete her hundred years so early? What was her illness? They said she had an operation."

"Yes, Aunt, she had an operation. They operate on so many people; it is my fate," Shekhar said with a heavy heart.

"The house needs a lady. One cannot imagine the misery of a house without one. We don't realize it when she is around."

Shekhar did not reply. There was no point in digging into the distressing past.

Krishnaveni brightened up the next minute.

"Do you want coffee, or should I ask for milk?" Shekhar asked.

"We did not even brush our teeth. Why milk? We will have coffee." She went into the room followed by Prabha.

"Look, take a central parting and put a big bindi and cover your shoulders with the pallav. Don't sit crunched up in a corner. Go all over the house with some cheer and interest. Shekhar is old-fashioned, so get close to the child also." Krishnaveni was advising Prabha with her worldly wisdom.

"Go, Grandma, you are always preaching to me."

"I am not preaching. After your two older sisters' marriages, your father is not solvent yet. What can he do for you? But it is only if he consents. Take some interest in the kitchen also."

"I am not good at all these things." Prabha was reluctant.

"How can you say that?"

Krishnaveni's husband was a police inspector. He had died suddenly of a heart attack, even before being eligible for pension or before his two sons could grow up. She raised and educated both of them and made them productive men. The older was Chalapati, and the younger, Sitaram. The older had five girls and then a boy. Sitaram had no children. Krishnaveni lived with her oldest son, Chalapati.

Krishnaveni and Prabha washed their faces and came to the dining table. Shekhar had Raghu and Rambabu on either side and was feeding them *upma*.

*Raghu is fine, but from where did this Rambabu turn up?*

"Poor fellow is struggling; go sit next to Raghu and feed him. What are you watching?" Krishnaveni nudged Prabha.

"No, it is all right. He has finished eating," replied Shekhar.

"I don't know how you are going to raise him without a woman's touch," she said.

"Aunt, did you not raise your children? In the same way, can I not raise these two boys?"

*These two boys? Who is this hoodlum? Who is Rambabu to Shekhar? How is he related? Sounds suspicious.* She decided to enquire into the matter.

"You have no problem. You are a man and will get

married royally. You will get a lady for the house. We are women. We are prisoners of this society. Everything is a hindrance and an obstacle. If we talk too much, we get criticized."

"Aunt, I have decided not to get married."

"You want to struggle like this, without marriage?"

"No, I am not struggling."

"That is what you will say now. After a while, when you are fed up with this lonely life, you will get married."

"Lonely! Me! I have these two boys with me."

"As you please," she said and twitched her mouth in disdain.

The next morning, both the children went to school. As usual, Malati went to the office room, minded her business, and returned to her room. Shekhar went to work.

Shekhar had said the previous day that he was definitely not getting married. *It was of no use in bringing Prabha along,* thought his aunt. *Other than that, this Rambabu shows up like a stick in the drink. Why is Shekhar treating this Rambabu like his own son? No one knows better than the servants in the house all the details and implications of a household. I will find out today.*

Krishnaveni was curious. She went to the veranda where the cook and Adamma were relaxing. She joined them and sat down, leaning against the wall.

"Adamma, I am asking in ignorance: Who are this mother and daughter staying in this room? Why is Shekhar pampering Rambabu so much? He is fussing over him more than his own child," Aunt asked with a face showing a big question mark.

"Ask us, Aunt. We also do not know." They were watching the aunt's reaction. "One evening Malati came. She and the master had a private conversation, and he got the room cleaned that very evening. The next day, these three arrived," said Adamma, anticipating the aunt's surprise.

Krishnaveni suspected a relationship between the two.

"Did they come here after the lady passed or before she passed away?" the aunt asked like a lawyer's interrogation.

"Why would they come earlier? They came afterwards," piped in the cook.

"That means they must have stayed elsewhere until the lady passed. Poor man. He brought them home after she was gone." Krishnaveni had studied the matter in her worldly wisdom and came to an easy conclusion. Adamma and the cook looked at each other and smirked.

"If you, as a family member, say it, it is all right. How can we, as servants, say these things?" Adamma opined.

"What is this, keeping Rambabu next to him and feeding him? Is he paying Malati for working in the office?"

"What salary! All their expenses are being paid."

Krishnaveni felt as if insects were crawling all over her body. She decided that she should take Prabha and get away from here as early as possible. I thought I would get him happily married, but this looks like a hell hole. She would inform Shekhar and plan to leave the next day. She was not going to stay a minute longer in this house of sin.

The world is bad. If you help someone, it is misunderstood. This rotten world. That afternoon, Adamma brought the children home from school. Krishnaveni looked at Rambabu with piercing eyes.

"Hey, kid, who is your father?"

"Who? I don't know," he said and ran away.

She waited for Shekhar. He came home at six in the evening. The cook brought the coffee and tiffin and kept it in front of him. Aunt was sitting across.

"Aunt, have you had your coffee and tiffin?" Shekhar asked.

"Yes, we all have had it."

"Did both the kids eat?"

"Yes, the TWO of them have eaten," she said with emphasis on the two.

Shekhar was surprised at her curtness. *Why does she dislike children so much?*

"We are planning to leave by tomorrow's train," she said.

"Why must you go so soon?"

"I am not feeling well at all. Your wife died more than two years ago. I should have come within the first ten days, but it materialized now. My health is not like it used to be." She acted weak and tired.

Krishnaveni and Prabha left the next day.

# Chapter Forty-one

Days became weeks, and weeks became months. Time was moving like a consuming flame. Everyone was growing up. Adamma's question was haunting Malati. *After he grows up and gets wiser, my son may ask me the question, "Who is my father?" What answer can I give him?*

# Chapter Forty-two

Three years earlier, Srihari Rao had speculated that Sarojini and Bhaskar's wedding was a sure thing. He had invited Raja Rao, his wife, and son to his home. Lalita thought that this alliance, coming from a rich family, should definitely come through and made many determined efforts to have it materialize, but she was not able to convince Bhaskar. Raja Rao wrote to Srihari Rao. The day Srihari received the letter, he was like a firecracker.

"What is it that they have that they are so arrogant?" he roared at everyone. When all his money belonged to his daughter, why wouldn't they accept? Money was not enticing enough for them? Even their ancestors would have descended from heaven for the money. He was defeated. He was hurt, but after a while, he resigned himself to the fact.

Sarojini buried her dreams within her. She was unhappy when alone. She stopped meeting Bhaskar at the beach. We attempt many things, but they all do not succeed.

"She is still childish and is unable to forget him,"

Srihari told his wife, Meena, who was depressed. Sarojini rejected many proposals of marriage.

"You are the one who spoiled her. You built up all her hopes," said Meena.

"Our wishes will be granted only if God also favors us," was Srihari Rao's reply.

Everyone presumed that Bhaskar and Sarojini would get married. Meena nagged her husband that her daughter was still unmarried.

"Why are you taunting me? I have been defeated. I realized that you cannot buy hearts and minds with money. These youngsters have taught me that values have changed. In my time, whomever our parents wanted us to marry, we did so blindly, like a trained bull shaking its head. Yes, those days are gone."

# Chapter Forty-three

Many years went by, and Bhaskar's parents were unable to convince him to marry. They left him alone, saying that his destiny would be fulfilled and could not be changed. Rajarao became reconciled to that fact. But Lalita was not able to give up easily. At every opportunity, she would bring up the topic. He did not want the alliance of Seshagiri Rao's daughter. He refused Sarojini. Each day, Bhaskar would go to the hospital and, later in the evening, go to the beach. He would meet his parents at dinner, and each retired to their rooms after that. This was the routine in Raja Rao's house.

One day, Bhaskar came home early at three in the afternoon. He sat at the dining table and asked the cook to serve him. Not to lose this opportunity, Lalita drew up a chair and sat next to him.

"Bhaskaru," she said endearingly.

He looked at her, questioning.

"You came early today."

"We had three operations today. For some reason, one got cancelled."

"When you came home early, I thought that may be you were not feeling well. I don't know; I don't like what is going on with you."

"Why? What is wrong with me?"

"Maybe if you marry a girl of your liking—"

"I thought you forgot the subject of marriage. I don't plan to get married."

"Are you going to be alone like this all your life?"

"So what?"

"I will ask you something; tell me."

"What is it?"

"Are you in love with anyone?"

"Why? Cannot I fall in love?"

"Not that you should not. If you tell us who she is, we will do our part and get you married in all pomp and splendor."

"There is no need for you to get involved in my marriage," he said firmly.

"Why such an extreme? Tell me one thing; will you marry Malati?" she asked, unabashed.

"Malati! Where is Malati? They left without informing us. You and father showed affection and respect, and they left without even informing. All right, Malati left. Couldn't she have written a letter? I now know very clearly that Malati does not want to marry me." Bhaskar was indignant.

Every word spoken by Bhaskar went like a spear, deep into Lalita's heart.

*He thinks that she did not write. Malati must have become a mother by now. My son's blood. I hope they did not leave him in an orphanage. What else will they do with the child? If our society knows that Malati is a mother, she cannot get married. Purna is always planning ahead, or did she cheat me at the outset? Lalita was very nervous.*

*Maybe I am the cause of Bhaskar's bitterness. I am to blame for everything. I am the one who wished Purna and Malati to go far away. Now where are they? I wonder. It has been some years since they left. By this time, Malati might be married and a mother to a couple of kids.*

# Chapter Forty-four

It was six in the evening, and Shekhar returned home. Raghu was not at home but was playing in Purna's room. That he was not alone and was playing with Rambabu made Shekhar happy. Adamma thought that Shekhar would be angry at her for letting Raghu play with the tenants.

"He does not listen. He always wants to be in their room," said Adamma, sheltering herself.

"Let him be; it does not matter," said Shekhar.

"There is no proper ventilation in that room."

"Then ask Rambabu to come here," he said, removing his coat.

"On hearing his father's voice, Raghu ran into the house, followed by Rambabu.

"Raghu, did you drink your milk?"

"No, Adamma did not give me," he said, looking at her.

"They are inside the room all the time and will not come out, even when asked to," she said defensively.

"If they don't come out, you can go in and give them the milk," Shekhar suggested.

"If I take a glass of milk into the room, Rambabu snatches it away."

"You can give him also."

"Yes, I can." Adamma paled. "I suppose I have to raise him also. I have no choice." She grimaced and brought two glasses of milk and gave it to them to drink.

"Adamma, please polish his shoes. They look very dusty," Shekhar said and went into his room.

"Yes, sir." Adamma brought Raghu's shoes and started polishing them. Rambabu ran to his room and brought his shoes.

"Polish these also," he said.

"Ask your mother to do it," she replied, irritated.

"There is no polish at home."

"If you don't have any, then buy some," she said sternly.

"Why? Why are you quarrelling?" asked Raghu.

"I asked her to polish my shoes, and she said to ask my mother," Rambabu replied, hurt.

"What, Adamma?" Raghu said fiercely.

"No, master, I said it jokingly." Both the children were close, and Adamma was envious. *Why is Ayya showing so much respect for someone off the streets?* she muttered.

It was the routine for Malati to give Rambabu his lunch wrapped in paper to take to school. Adamma gave Raghu his lunch in a steel container. They went together in the car with Shekhar, and when school was over, Adamma brought both the kids home.

One day Raghu was ready and was waiting at the car. Rambabu did not come.

"Adamma, go and enquire," said Shekhar.

Adamma went to Malati's room.

"Malatamma, if Rambabu is not going to school, could you not inform us?" she said.

"That's not it. I packed his bread in a paper, and he lost it. So mother has gone to the bazaar to buy some more bread. She will be right back."

"Shouldn't you check earlier if there is any bread in the house? For your carelessness, master is scolding me."

Malati was tense but did not react.

"There she is," Malati said and quickly wrapped up a parcel and sent Rambabu to the car.

Shekhar observed all this, and in the evening, he took both the kids to Kathiawar General Store on Abid Road and bought a steel tiffin carrier and a book bag for Rambabu. He also bought them some toys, shopped for some clothes, and came home. Both the children were delighted. Rambabu ran to his mother with his new clothes, toys, and other things.

"Amma! Raghu's father bought me these clothes, this tiffin box, and the bag. From tomorrow, he said we could play in the garden, and he got us a ball. Here, see, he also bought Raghu all this. Did you see this car? You turn this key and it runs."

With great delight, he showed his mother his new acquisitions, taking them out one by one. Purna was stunned. Raghu was standing near the door, forlorn.

"Raghu, come in. Where's your car and your ball?" asked Malati.

"They are at home. Adamma said not to bring them here."

"Not bring them here?"

"Yes. Shall I bring them?" he perked up.

"No, I will come myself," said Malati and walked into the house.

Raghu, Rambabu, and Malati walked into the house. Adamma followed them. Both the kids were racing their cars. Adamma stood near the door, muttering. Malati ignored Adamma's pecking and played with the children. When Shekhar arrived, Malati took Rambabu and went back into her room.

# Chapter Forty-five

Driver Venkiah, the cook, Adamma, the servant boy, and Narasimhulu were all drinking hot coffee in the veranda adjacent to the kitchen.

"Last evening, Master went to the bazaar and bought both the kids do you know how many toys and clothes? Somewhere they lucked out and came here. They are blessed," said Venkiah enthusiastically.

"That Rambabu is incorrigible. You tell Raghu, and he listens. Rambabu is stubborn. He tries to order me around. Is HIS father paying me?" joined Adamma.

"If he has a father to give you money!" said the cook, drinking his hot coffee.

"I asked the mother one day when her son-in-law was coming," Adamma refueled.

"What did she say?" said Narasimhulu eagerly.

"'I don't know when he will come,' she said unhesitatingly."

"I don't think she is married. She does not have the thali round her neck," the cook said lecherously.

"But the master has his eye on Malatamma," said Narasimhulu bravely.

"Yes, how do you know?" asked Venkiah indignantly.

"How do I know? When he is working in the office, Ramayya has been noticing."

"Did Ramayya tell you?" asked Venkiah with twice the indignation.

"Yes, Ramayya told me. Such things, cannot be hidden."

"What did he tell you?" demanded Venkiah.

"What did he tell me? 'I am the one who does all the work, and she gets paid for it,'" Narasimhulu replied.

"Why does he say that about her not working? She goes to the office every morning without fail." Venkiah's indignation did not diminish.

"Why wouldn't she go? That long braid, those buttery eyes, she can make anyone unconscious. Otherwise, will Master allow that Rambabu to be so familiar?" said Adamma, as if she was the only wise one. "For whom is all this nudging in the dark?"

"Why cannot she just vacate the room and walk into the house?" said the cook, solving the problem.

"Soon we will witness that also," said Adamma, making a face.

"He does not have a wife, she does not have a husband, why can't they choose an auspicious day and get married?" Narasimhulu passed judgment.

"Do you know how that Rambabu talks to me?" said Adamma.

"What did he say?" the cook prodded her, setting his coffee cup down.

"What did he say? What does he not say? One day when he was naughty, I scolded him. 'You are not my mother to scold me.'" Adamma looked at each one to note their reaction.

"Anyone criticizing Master will lose their eyes. Malati is like fire, and he is large-hearted. He is taking care of two women, as they were in trouble. Is that wrong?" said Venkiah harmonizing the conversation.

As Venkiah was not in agreement with the rest, they repressed their opinion. "It is not our business. They are lucky and happened to turn up here," said Adamma, retreating. The three left with their coffee glasses. Venkiah was alone and pensive.

"Venkiah." There was a call from inside, and he left the glass there and ran in. As he left Adamma, the cook and Narasimhulu returned.

# Chapter Forty-six

Whenever Bhaskar sat on the beach, he remembered Malati. *Will we ever meet again in this life? If not in this life—?* The very thought twisted his heart. He would spend hours staring into the ocean. Now and again, Sarojini would come to the beach. He would run into her occasionally at the hospital. She would meet him cheerily on some pretext. She was unable to get him out of her heart and did not even try to, but worshipped him. Her father brought her many alliances, which she rejected, such that he got fed up and gave up looking, philosophizing that marriage was not necessary.

Nowadays, Sarojini did not go to the beach. Many were unhappy because of Bhaskar. The girl he promised to marry had distanced herself. Rejected, Sarojini was heartbroken with no hope or cheer, but in pure misery. His parents were suffering as there was no daughter-in-law in the house. They wanted Bhaskar to get married, live a domestic life, and produce an heir. That was their only desire.

But they did not seem to realize that marriage is associated with love. Whether you will love after marriage or hate each other was written on your forehead the day you were born. This is what the elders say when they shower blessings on you with colored rice at the wedding. The elders are the ones to fix the match. They bargain for money and dowry and also bless for a good destiny. With these profound thoughts, Bhaskar went back home on his scooter.

As he reached home, he found the car racing out of the gate like an arrow. *Where is it going in a rush?* he wondered.

"Bhaskar! Have you come? Your father is not well. You were late in coming home. I have sent the car for the doctor." Lalita was agitated.

Bhaskar was shocked on hearing the news. His father lay in bed, looking tired. He was breathing rapidly and pouring sweat. Bhaskar gently wiped him with the towel next to him. Raja Rao opened his eyes and smiled affectionately at his son. Bhaskar was unhappy that his father was crumbling and that he was troubled. The car returned along with the doctor, who examined Raja Rao. Bhaskar and the doctor stepped out of the room.

"Dr. Bhaskar, what is it that you do not know? He has to take a lot of rest. It is a good idea to hospitalize him," he said and looked to Bhaskar for his opinion. Bhaskar, in turn, looked at his mother.

"No, it's all right. It will settle itself. He is much better than earlier. An hour ago, he was writhing with pain in the chest. He is much better now. Why hospitalize for a trivial matter?" Lalita struck out the doctor's advice.

To prove that Lalita was wrong, Raja Rao's pain increased that night. As he was in great distress, Lalita and Bhaskar unanimously agreed to take him to the hospital and took him by car.

There he was placed on a trolley and taken to his room. The oxygen given through the tube gave some comfort to his heart. With the injections that were given, he had a good rest. Bhaskar stayed the whole night with him. He asked his mother to go home and return in the morning.

As his father was admitted in the hospital where he worked, Bhaskar was not inconvenienced. Mother and son were taking turns to be with Raja Rao. Day by day he improved, and in ten days, he went home. Raja Rao was placed on dietary restrictions. Bhaskar came home directly after work to attend to his father. Both parents were impressed and delighted at the care and effort put in by their son. They rejoiced inwardly.

Lalita was rattled by her husband's illness. Fear took hold of her. She lost her strength and courage. She was nervous. She stopped her stinging remarks. On the other hand, she was very gentle and kind. Raja Rao also was shaken up with this heart condition. It was as if the God of Death told him, "I am near you."

Raja Rao was brooding. He asked for Subbiah so that he could draw up his will. Subbiah arrived and stood in front of him, but Raja Rao had not noticed, as his eyes were closed. In a while he opened them and saw Subbiah for the first time since coming home from the hospital. On seeing him, Raja Rao broke down and wiped his tears in embarrassment. Subbiah blotted his own tears.

"Subbiah," he cried in a weak voice.

"Sir," said Subbiah, coming closer.

"Take the car and bring my friend Iswar Rao, the

lawyer. I need to write my will."

"As you say. I shall leave right away," said Subbiah and left. Bhaskar entered on hearing some sound. Raja Rao opened his eyes.

"Bhaskar, come and sit here."

He pulled up a chair close to his father's bed. There was a brief silence.

"I have asked for Iswar Rao. I want to write my will. This house and money, half of it is yours. The money that comes from selling the lands and any other money in the form of jewelry, this other half should go to Purna or Malati. Mother will be under your care and protection. This is what I have decided. What do you think?"

"We don't know where Purna and Malati are."

"Then I will write everything to you. Anytime you happen to meet them, tell them this was my wish and give them the money."

"Did you ask for me?" said Iswar Rao entering the room.

"Yes, I did."

"Why are you lying down? Are you not well?"

"Recently, I was seriously ill."

"*Hayyo*, I did not know."

"Now I am a little better. So far, I have not written my will and have decided to write one. The details Bhaskar will tell you. You write it up and bring it for my signature."

"All right, I will bring it in a couple of days. You take care of your health," said Iswar Rao and left.

After some days, Raja Rao signed his will in the presence of two witnesses. He was still in bed. He was allowed to walk around the room, and he did that without any trouble.

One morning he woke up and washed his face and lay down.

"Lalita," he called to his wife.

"What, dear?" She went near him.

"You have stopped giving me coffee because the doctor asked you not to, isn't it?" he said jokingly.

"Yes, if the doctor forbade it."

"Today I am feeling very tired. Maybe you can give a small glass, just for today," he begged.

"All right," she said and left the room.

She brought back a small glass of coffee and noticed a queer look on her husband's face.

"Bhaskar!" she screamed.

"What, mother?" He came running. In the meantime, Bhaskar's father and Lalita's husband had left all his dear ones and gone to the other world. Lalita was petrified. Bhaskar drew her close to him and laid a hand on her shoulder. She drooped over him and sobbed.

The news that Raja Rao had passed crawled everywhere in the neighborhood. Everyone visited. Everybody talked. "He asked for coffee but died without drinking it." They repeated themselves.

All the required last rites were performed with all honors to his mother's satisfaction.

After her husband passed away, there was a change in Lalita. She had not known any difficulties but only happiness. She was always the boss but never subordinate. Bhaskar was distressed at the change in his mother. He did not go to work for a month after his father died. From the time his father was sick, he did not go to the beach. When the month was over, he rejoined duty. He would go to the hospital and come straight home to keep his mother company. He would discuss every matter with her and conducted the household matters according to her wishes. In the evening, he would discuss with Subbiah issues about the business. Lalita was thrilled and proud of her son, who was competent in every aspect. But that he was not married bothered her.

Bhaskar was transferred from Vizag to the big hospital in Hyderabad. He told his mother about it. She was pleased, as she had wanted to move out of Vizag since the death of her husband. The business on the main road was sold, and Lalita and Bhaskar moved to Hyderabad.

# Chapter Forty-seven

The river of time does not wait for anyone. Raghu and Rambabu were growing up. Raghu obtained a seat in the medical college, and Shekhar was thrilled. Rambabu would say, "I will grow up and be like you. I will go to court." Shekhar was pleased that Rambabu was always in the big house eating, playing, and studying, but at night he would go back to his mother's room.

Shekhar was elated that the two boys were like brothers. He got suits stitched for the both of them. The tailor folded them well, packed them in two cardboard boxes, and handed it over. Rambabu took the box and undid the bow on the box, unfolded his suit, and showed it to his mother.

"Raghu has one just like this, except that his tie is different," he said enthusiastically.

"It is very nice. Keep it back carefully in the box," Malati said.

"No, mother, I am going to hang it up in Raghu's cupboard."

"Did you ask Raghu?"

"I did not ask. Raghu told me to store my clothes in his cupboard."

"Then it is all right."

"I will take my shirts also. Adamma will iron them."

He opened his mother's box and took out some clothes. He found Bhaskar's photo. Squinting his eyes, he stared at it for a few minutes. Malati did not notice this.

"Who is this, Mother?" he asked. She turned around.

"What can I tell you?" she said sadly.

"Is it Father?"

"Not that lucky."

"Then your father?"

"No."

"Then who? Can't you tell me?"

"He is my God!"

"God—means? Can't you tell me?" he begged.

"Not now. One day I will definitely tell you."

*When the circumstances are ready, I will tell you*, she thought to herself.

"I will take these clothes and keep them in Raghu's cupboard," Rambabu said and left with the clothes.

Rambabu opened Raghu's cupboard. Adamma came rushing after him.

"Why did you come to this room?" she asked sternly, as if asking a criminal.

"I am going to keep my clothes here," he said.

"No, you are taking something stealthily."

"Adamma!" he said with indignation.

"Rambabu is stealing something!" she bellowed.

Shekhar, Raghu, Malati, Purna, and the servants all came rushing in. Adamma said nothing.

Ram Babu was embarrassed.

"What happened?" roared Shekhar.

"I came to keep my suit in the cupboard." Rambabu looked at his mother.

"I told him to keep his clothes in my cupboard," Raghu said in explanation.

Adamma shuddered.

"Adamma, the children have grown up. They do not need an ayah. You can quit work," Shekhar said sternly.

Until now, Malati had no occasion to talk to Shekhar.

"Adamma need not go; we will leave," she said bravely.

"Amma, both the boys are grown up. It is not necessary for Adamma to stay," said Shekhar firmly and walked out.

One by one, they slowly slid out of the room. Malati went to her room and sobbed. That night, Rambabu ate with his mother and stayed with her. Adamma packed her belongings and left in an auto.

# Chapter Forty-eight

Time went back and moved forward. Raghu completed his medical studies and obtained the MBBS degree. Rambabu finished his BA and completed law school. He worked along with Shekhar at the courthouse. Shekhar took care of him in every way so that he did not feel like a fatherless child. All arrangements were made and dues were paid to become an advocate. The next morning, Rambabu would be enrolled in the bar.

He dressed up neatly and, before going to court, went to his mother and fell at her feet. She blessed him with pride. He touched Purna's feet to his eyes. She raised him up and said, "Prostrate before Ayyagaru. He is our God and protector."

Rambabu went to Shekhar and prostrated full length, surrendering at his feet in gratitude. Shekhar raised him up with joy and hugged him.

On seeing that, Ramayya thought, *There must be a connection from the previous birth, or else why would a street urchin get so much respect from Shekhar?* He was envious of this abundance of love.

"All these days, his name was Rambabu, but from now on, his name will be Rama Rao," announced Shekhar.

They proudly hung a board on the wall of the gate in both English and Telugu that said Rama Rao, BA, BL. The other side had Shekhar's name. So whenever Purna and Malati passed the gate, they would stop to read the board and enter the house. In their hearts, they raised their hands to Shekhar in gratitude. They could never repay him for many generations.

Days were flying by.

# Chapter Forty-nine

Bhaskar reached Hyderabad with his mother and joined duty. Now and again, Malati would sneak into his heart. He thought of Malati frequently and thought that she must have married someone else and was living happily with a husband and children. *These women are lucky. They can love whoever ties the thali around their necks. To love one and have children by another is a skill women learn from birth. Women, the low-life, the despicable race.* He was sickened.

One day in the hospital he met Sarojini, and both were surprised.

"Why are you here? I hope none of your people are admitted here as a patient?" she asked, worried.

"No, I have been transferred here."

"Yes, one of the surgeons who used to be here has gone to America on leave. I think you are replacing him."

"Yes."

"When did you come to town?"

"About a month ago."

"You came alone or—"

"I and my mother."

"Father?"

"He's gone."

"Hayyo."

"I'll see you."

Bhaskar did not want to prolong the conversation. Sarojini followed him with her eyes until he disappeared.

This is called divine intervention. She was finding it difficult to forget him, and for them to meet again and work in the same hospital! But it looked like he had been hardened to the philosophy of an ascetic. "I and my mother" means there is no wife.

*Probably not married yet,* she thought. *Would he have been a bachelor all these years? Maybe not. Would his parents have allowed him to stay unmarried? Nothing wrong with him; I am sure he has gotten married. She might have gone home to her parents for childbirth. My madness. Why should I get so flustered when I see him? Why these hopes and disappointments? When I see him next time, I will ask him, "Are you married?" Supposing he does not reply and turns his face away?*

Sarojini entered the ward to see her patients.

# Chapter Fifty

Shekhar's practice picked up very well, and work at the office had increased. Ramayya was struggling to get the typed papers ready for Shekhar. He was scolding Malati as if it was all her fault. Even after all these years, she was irresponsible and inefficient. Malati would wipe her tears and carefully complete tasks assigned to her. She did not even tell her mother about the hassles in the office. Ramayya did not touch the typewriter once Malati joined the office. But he was intolerant of her. He could not understand why. He never mentioned to Shekhar that work was too much and that he needed help. So why was she appointed? He was questioning himself.

*Where did she come from? She was pretty and sweet and attractive too. I, in my old age, feel thrilled on seeing her. What of Shekhar, who is much younger? Poor man. His wife died. If he is able to control himself, it is amazing. Brahma in his benevolence must have sent Malati here to him.*

Shekhar was at the table writing. He asked Ramayya for some papers.

"They are not yet ready," he replied to Shekhar. "Malatamma! Ayya is inconvenienced, as you have not typed the papers in time. No work will get done at this rate," he said loudly.

"Ramayya, it is your duty to keep the papers ready on my desk," said Shekhar sternly.

"I gave them all to her," he stammered.

"So where are they?"

"She has not got them ready yet."

Malati heard him. "Ramayya garu, what is it that you asked me that I have not done?" She bravely stood her ground.

Ramayya was in a bind. *She came unexpectedly sharp as a needle. Today her son also is an advocate, so why would she not be bold? It is better for me to calm down.*

"I thought I gave you the papers; I am sorry."

There was minor friction happening all the time. Ramayya kept scratching his head, and Malati bent her head and withdrew.

The next day after this encounter, Malati, on her way to the bathroom, felt dizzy and fell down. Purna caught her in time. She walked her slowly and had her lie on the bed. She gave her some coffee from a small glass, and she seemed to recover.

Ramayya was getting frustrated that Malati had not come to the office. The news that Malati felt dizzy reached the office. Shekhar decided that until Malati returned to work, Ramayya would take care of all office matters. Purna was with her daughter all day. Rambabu finished his daily work and stayed with his mother.

"How are you feeling, Mother? Do you want me to stay with you?"

"I just felt dizzy. There is nothing to it. You go attend to your work," Malati objected. Purna sat with Malati near the bed, her heart full of memories of a lifetime.

"What, Mother? You seem to be thinking about something," said Malati.

"Because you were born of me, you have had nothing but trouble. Your whole life has been in tears. A lonely life, you have not enjoyed any of the joys of life. If your father were alive, your life might have been totally different."

Malati took her mother's hand in hers.

"Mother, do not worry about me at all. I am not suffering as much as you think. You proved that motherhood is the alms given to a woman by God. I have considered it to be my calling to raise Rambabu into a productive human being. I have no other desires. Don't destroy yourself. We have Rambabu. What else do we want?" she said gravely. Purna's eyes were filled with tears.

"Mother, do not suffer because of me. Marriage has evaded this unlucky one, but I have experienced the beauty, happiness, and purity that love can give. I have kept my Bava safely in my heart and am worshipping him. Destiny has been stubborn but has not touched my love. I will face life with stubbornness. When Rambabu was born, with his cry, he begged, 'Don't throw me away.' In my interest and for my happiness, you wanted the innocent babe, one who knows no sin, to be given away to an orphanage. Anyway, he does not have a father. I did not want him to be distanced from a mother too. That was unjust. I did not want to punish him by being afraid of society. My heart told me that very strongly. You have helped me and supported me in every way, and that is enough for me. Whenever Rambabu calls me Mother, I feel that life is tapping me and telling me that by motherhood my life has not been wasted. When he calls you Grandma, I realize that we are not destitute.

The satisfaction that I did not get with marriage, that happiness I have gotten from my child. With determination, I have obtained that happiness. Do not worry about me. What else can we wish for?"

The mother could not contain her sorrow and fell over Malati and cried. Both their faces were covered with tears. No words are sufficient to fathom what was in their hearts.

"I said, 'What else is there for us to wish for?' There is one wish that has been planted deeply and strongly in my heart. I have to meet Bava and ask, 'Is there so much treachery in you? Here is your son.' I have to hand over his child to him."

"What are you thinking, dear? Did he reply at least to one of your letters?"

"Maybe he did not get them."

"Why wouldn't he get them? I don't believe that not even one letter has reached him," said Purna.

"If you blame him, I cannot bear it," Malati said and turned over to the other side of the bed. Purna left the room.

# Chapter Fifty-one

From the time Malati felt dizzy and fell, she did not go to the office. Ramayya complained. A month later, Malati died in her sleep. She felt as if she had lived enough, and her soul left the body liberated. Purna felt as if her life was over. Rambabu was inconsolable. He thought that more investigations should have been done the day she felt dizzy. She died suddenly, as it was undiagnosed. He was agitated. He was sad that he was careless. She should have been taken to a doctor earlier.

Milk boiled over, or a lost life will not return. Purna's sorrow was heart-breaking. Rambabu performed all the rites and rituals according to tradition with a heavy heart that was filled with gratitude.

With time, the sorrow quieted down. After twenty days, Shekhar asked him to come to court. He went with his grandmother's permission. Purna was going out of her mind without Malati. The only one left was her grandson. Rambabu was with Shekhar all the time except at night. Before going to work, he would always bid his grandmother goodbye.

# Chapter Fifty-two

It was a Sunday, and everyone was at home until the afternoon. Raghu and Rambabu went to the three o'clock matinee. Shekhar came into the hall and leisurely opened the morning paper. Coffee and tiffin were placed on the table by the cook. On turning the second page, whatever it was that he read caused Shekhar to rush inside and pull the wallet from his coat pocket. He pulled out a ticket and compared the numbers on the ticket with the winning numbers in the paper. He was inundated with joy.

"Narasimhulu!" he shouted and ran into the room.

"Do you know which cinema the two have gone to?"

"Yes, I do."

"Then call the cinema hall and check if the movie is over."

"Yes, I will." He came back into the room. "The show finished over half an hour ago." The phone rang, and Narasimhulu answered the phone.

"Sir, you have a call from Madras."

"Call from Madras?" he said and left the room.

"Hullo! Is that you? What's up? Yes, I also just saw the paper. Yes, that's the number. How did you know? I will mail you the tickets by registered post. Yes, sure, I will tell them. Many thanks. Is that all? Shall I hang up?" he said, then hung up.

Raghu and Rambabu came home.

"Rambabu, congratulations! You have won ten lakhs in the lottery," Shekhar said enthusiastically.

"What? Me? Lottery?" He was paralyzed.

"Yes. One day at court, they were selling Tamilnadu lottery tickets. I bought a couple in your names. Rambabu's ticket—you have won ten lakhs. Here is the paper. Just now, my friend from Madras also called me. If we mail him the tickets, he will arrange to validate them."

Raghu gave Rambabu a big hug.

"I am all confused," said Rambabu softly.

"What are you going to do with the ten lakhs?" asked Raghu.

"Since Ayya bought the tickets, the money is his, not mine," Rambabu said dutifully.

"Go and tell your grandma about this."

Rambabu rushed to Purna.

"What is it? What is the hurry?" said Purna.

"If I am not rushed, what else is it? I have won ten lakhs in the lottery!"

"For you and me, a lakh (laksha)? It is Sri Rama's protection (raksha)."

Raghu entered. "Ammamma, what is Rambabu going to do with all that money?"

"What? Why are you joking with me?"

"It is not a joke," they both said.

"Is it true?" she said, looking straight at them.

"Yes," said Raghu.

Just as they had rushed into Purna's room, they rushed out again.

"Tomorrow we will send the tickets to Madras by registered post," said Shekhar.

Everyone was immersed in happiness. Ten lakhs was no joke. All the servants thought that Rambabu was a very lucky boy. Or else why would he come to this house?

The next day, on the way to the high court, they stopped at the post office and sent the ticket to Madras by registered post. Within a week, Rambabu received the money by bank draft. The following day, Shekhar and Rambabu went to the bank and cashed it. The people at the bank looked at Rambabu with surprise for having won the lottery. Some of the workers congratulated him.

Shekhar mulled it over and bought a piece of land close to his house and planned to build a nursing home. He informed Raghu and Rambabu. Since the money came in Rambabu's name, they decided to name the nursing home after his mother. The land was bought, and the contract for the construction of the building was given to a friend of Shekhar. On an auspicious day they laid the foundation stone. Day by day, the building took shape. Since there was no want of money, the building was constructed quickly. Every evening Shekhar, Raghu, and Rambabu would go to the construction site and watch the progress until dark.

The nursing home, with modern conveniences and modern operation theatres, was completed. They decided to celebrate the opening in a grand manner. They named it "Matri Sri Home." They had a big photo of Malati and were going to put it up at the entrance on the inaugural day. They had printed invitations for the opening on Malati's second death anniversary.

Rambabu gave invitations to all the doctors and the bigwigs in town. Two ministers agreed to attend. One was to preside over the function and the other to unveil the portrait and speak. The nursing home was decorated with colored paper, flowers, and garlands. They tied streamers of mango leaves at the gate. Banana trees adorned the pillars of the gate.

On that inaugural day, the building was shining. The guests were to arrive. Raghu, Shekhar, and Rambabu were standing in the veranda. Venkiah and Ramayya were at the gate. The guests were arriving and alighting at the entrance. Officers, doctors, and dignitaries were sitting in the chairs under the shamiana. Cool drinks were being served by waiters dressed in white. Recorded music floated in the air. The two special invitees and the ministers who arrived sat in their assigned chairs. When everyone was seated, Rambabu read his prepared speech. He thanked the guests for accepting his invitation and specifically expressed his gratitude to the two ministers. Raghu garlanded the two, to much applause. The presiding minister expressed the need for such well-equipped nursing homes to serve the public. Not only was Rambabu providing a service to the sick, but also a memorial to his mother. Though he was young, he had lofty ideals for the larger good. This theme was repeated many times. Shekhar requested the second minister to unveil Malati's portrait. The minister pulled a red cord to uncover the portrait and received the appropriate applause.

Being one of the invitees, Bhaskar was astounded on seeing Malati's picture. His head was reeling. Malati's photo—that smiling face. Is he Malati's son? Did Malati get married? Who is this Shekhar? What is their relationship? How are they connected? Thoughts and questions flooded his brain without end and in long orations. Everyone praised Rambabu as the ideal son, said how blessed the mother was, gave accolades, and a lot more. Shekhar gave the vote of thanks to all the guests who graced the occasion. The ministers were especially thanked, and everyone was escorted to their vehicles by Shekhar, Raghu, and Rambabu. The function concluded.

Bhaskar slumped in his chair. He was all alone at the venue. Rambabu went up to him and enquired if he felt unwell. Bhaskar looked into Rambabu's eyes.

"Come inside. Seems like you are unwell. You can have a little coffee," Rambabu entreated. Bhaskar silently followed him inside. Having seated him restfully on a sofa, Rambabu brought him a glass of coffee and sat down next to Bhaskar.

"Today's function went off very well," said Bhaskar.

"Everything is Ayya's arrangements."

"How are you related to Shekhar Rao?"

"He is my father."

"Ah!" he said, surprised.

"Yes, when my mother had nowhere to go, he took her in, as also her mother and me, and watched over us. He raised me, loved me, and made me a useful man in society. This large-hearted man, he is the God who nurtured me and my mother."

"So he is your father—? Bhaskar questioned.

"He watched over me more than his own son and is

a great man," said Rambabu.

"That means you are not his biological son."

"I am telling you he is the God who protected me. I salute him every day," he said and joined his hands and raised them in the air.

"He is lucky to have been able to nourish you and your mother. I am a sinner who has been deprived of these dreams, bonds, and joys. Malati is your mother?"

"Not Malati, say Malatamma. Yes, she is my mother."

*How respectful he is to his mother,* thought Bhaskar.

"How long is it since your mother died?" asked Bhaskar, drinking his coffee.

"Exactly two years to the day. That is why we had this inauguration today as a memorial to her."

*Where did all this money come from? If it is Shekhar's money, why did he name it after Malati?* Bhaskar's mind was confused. He also had some unwarranted thoughts, but consoled himself.

"I am your mother's Bava," Bhaskar said boldly.

"On seeing you, I guessed that you were someone close."

Bhaskar paled. "How did you know?" he said, surprised.

"My mother has a photo of you in your younger days. I still have it. One day I saw it and asked her who it was. 'Don't ask me that one question, child,' she said. She had tears in her eyes. That's why I did not raise that question again."

Bhaskar left the empty glass on the table, his face covered with sorrow.

"You come inside. You can meet Ayya and Raghu." He took Bhaskar into Shekhar's room.

"Namaskar, please sit down," said Shekhar.

"Namaskar," Bhaskar said, returning the greeting. "I came for the inauguration of your nursing home today," he said and drew a chair and sat down.

"Many thanks."

"I saw Rambabu's mother's photo. She is my paternal aunt's daughter. There was some domestic quarrel, and my aunt and she left the house."

"Yes. It is almost eighteen years ago. Rambabu must have been four years old. My bad luck, I lost my wife, and those were the days when I was overwhelmed and pained. His mother pleaded to me that she had no food to eat and no shade to stand under. Since I know the meaning of trouble, that very moment, I gave her a place to stay. My son Raghu lost his mother and was confused. So that my son would not be alone, I took them in. Raghu and Rambabu grew up like brothers. I wanted to build a nursing home for him, but I did not have the money. God has blessed our efforts. Rambabu unexpectedly won ten lakhs in the lottery. With that money, we built this home."

"Fate is strange," Bhaskar said, dejected. "That's the way it is. I shall leave." He got up.

Bhaskar could not stop his tears and went out of the room. Shekhar and Rambabu saw him off with sadness. Bhaskar turned around with second thoughts. "Is Rambabu's mother's mother, Purnamma, around?"

"Yes, she is here," said Rambabu.

"Can I meet her?"

"Sure," said Rambabu and led him inside to Purna's room.

Purna was working in the kitchen, burdened with old age and heartache. Her suffering made her stoop.

"Did your function go off well?" she asked Rambabu.

"Yes, it went off well. You did not want to come when I asked you to," he said angrily.

"Did you put up your mother's photo?"

"Yes, I did. Everyone said she must have been a very lucky mother to have a son like me. Look, someone has come to visit you."

"To see me! Do I still exist in this world for someone to want to see me?"

Bhaskar, still standing at the door, thought that this is the shape of sorrow.

"Auntie, I am Bhaskar." He came forward.

Purna's eyes were a little hazy these days. She looked at him closely. "Bhaskar." She flung her arms out in a hug with tears in her eyes.

She composed herself in a few minutes.

"God gave your aunt nothing but trouble. But he gave ME a long life. HE took Malati away, leaving me behind," she said, wiping her tears.

Bhaskar could not speak.

"How are your mother and father?" Purna asked.

"Father passed away."

"What? Brother has gone?"

"It is already a year now. He was miserable about your departure."

"Yes, he is very respectable. We left without informing him. Did he forgive us? Bhaskar, you have changed a lot. Are you in town?" Purna sent a volley of questions.

"Yes, we have been here for over a month. Aunt! Malati...." he said softly.

"Malati has left all of us," she said, wiping her tears.

"Forgive me, Aunt. I was anxious to know about

Malati. I am sorry. Forgive me."

"Malati loved you with all her heart. She was not able to reach out to the one she loved. She lived her whole life as a living corpse. She was brave outwardly. "If not in this world, I will meet my Bava in the next," she would say. This Rambabu is not anybody. He is your son. Your very own son!"

"Auntie!" He was motionless.

"Yes, it is. I will tell you Malati loved you and gave you her all. When she knew that she was pregnant, she wanted to inform you and went to your house." She stopped.

"She came to our house? And then?"

"Why do you want to know all that now? Let me tell you clearly. Rambabu is your biological son."

"Aunt, why did you leave without informing us?"

"Why?" She was contemplating and could not speak.

"Never mind, you had left, but you could have at least written to us."

"Yes we made a mistake," she said sarcastically.

"Because of your mistake, you separated me and my son from each other," he said sadly.

"We did not distance you. Malati wrote three or four letters, but you, did you reply? She would think about it every day and voice it every day. 'One day I will tell Bava, here is your son.' She wanted to gift him to you. Every time he called her 'Mother,' she suffered that he was not lucky enough to say 'Father.' Today he is my only solace. He cares for me like the apple of his eye. I will ask you what I should not. Are you married?" The last question was in a critical tone.

"Auntie, if I would have married, it would have been

Malati and none else. I promised her."

"*Hayyo*! What is this? Did your parents agree to this?"

"No. They did make attempts to fix me up. But they could not convince me."

"Bhaskar! Everyone has had lonely lives!"

"Ammamma." Rambabu came into the room.

"Child, this Bhaskar is not anybody. He is your father."

Rambabu looked at him cruelly.

"Yes, I am your father." Bhaskar went to embrace him. Rambabu stepped back.

"My father!" he said with contempt.

"All these years you did not know that you had a father, and I did not know that I have a son. Today is a blessed day that I am able to see you."

"Excuse me, Dr. Bhaskar. Ayya, who respected my mother, is my father. Who is a father? Not him who begets. The one who loved me and nurtured me and made me a respectable member of society is my father." Rambabu left the room, repulsed.

Purna was stunned. Bhaskar stood like a pillar for a few minutes and gradually left the room.

He started the car, his heart in turmoil. Circumstances were cruel to him. He was unable to bear the insult he received today. His own son rejected him. The hurt dug deep into his heart. Malati was no more. *Why am I still alive? If only I had known that I had a son. Hayyo! Why is fate testing me?* He reached home in disbelief, thoughts swirling in his head.

"Babu," said Lalita as she came to the front door. She saw his ghastly face and was afraid. "It is very late," she said.

"Yes, it did get late," he said absentmindedly.

He went into his room and slumped on the bed, rolling around in unbearable turmoil. He was undecided about telling his mother. He determined not to tell her. He was misunderstood. *I don't need anyone's sympathy. I have no one to claim as my own. My son cursed me and rejected me. I cannot bear this insult. I have to tell Rambabu that this was not my fault or else my soul will not rest in peace.*

Lalita was petrified on seeing Bhaskar that night. She was never discouraged before. She did not have the courage to say, "Babu, let's have dinner." Both of them starved that night.

# Chapter Fifty-three

The next morning, Bhaskar went to the hospital early, even before Lalita woke up. He completed all his jobs mechanically, attended to all the patients that he needed to, and wrote all the notes in the records that were required. It was very late by the time he reached home.

A week had passed by. All these days he had been anxious about Purna and Malati's whereabouts. Now he knew, but was still miserable. All these days there had been hope; now all his dreams were broken.

One day he went to bed saying that he was not feeling well. It was about eleven o'clock, and he got out of bed. He wandered about the room aimlessly. He picked up a piece of paper and a pen and wrote a letter and stepped out. His mother seemed to be sleeping in her room. He woke up the servant boy, who slept in the veranda.

"Tomorrow morning, go to the house in Khairatabad and give this letter to Rambabu, who lives at the back of the house."

He nodded his head. "Yes, sir," he said with sleepy

eyes.

"You must definitely go. This should reach him in the morning."

"Definitely. After I deliver it, I will let you know."

*'You will tell me, all right*, he thought.

He went back to his room without a sound. He injected himself, left the syringe on the side table, and went to sleep.

The next morning, Lalita entered the room. "Babu, how are you?" When she looked at his face, she knew some disaster had befallen him.

"Chukamma!" she yelled a terrible scream.

"What is it?" Chukkamma rushed in.

"Send the servant to fetch a doctor immediately."

"He is not here. He has gone to deliver a letter given by the young master. He left early this morning by auto."

"Why don't you go and bring the nearest doctor?"

Chukkamma, though old and slow, went in a hurry and brought the doctor in a few minutes. The doctor examined the empty syringe on the table at the side.

"Amma, there is nothing more I can do after he has taken this medicine," he said and looked at the dead body in despair.

The servant boy gave Bhaskar's letter to the servant Narasimhulu, who in turn gave it to Rambabu.

"Who will send me a letter so early in the morning?" Rambabu thought, and he read:

*To Chiranjeevi Rambabu,*

*My wholehearted love and blessings. I am sending you my will. Circumstances cruelly separated us. But I was able to cope with the strength and fortitude I received from your mother. I spent my whole life in the hope that I would meet her one day. Now that I know she is gone, I have no use for this life. For having existed as a living corpse all these years, I was finally able to meet you. That is enough for me. Your mother must have cursed me a lot, but I was not responsible for those circumstances. She left us without that knowledge. But what pierces me the most is that I distanced my son. I am not able to bear it and cannot accept it. By the time you get this letter, I will have passed on. I have only one wish. Please place the photo of me beside your mother's.*

*Nothing else.*

*Your father,*
*Bhaskar*

On reading the letter, Rambabu was terrified. Purna had just woken up and rubbed her eyes. "Ammamma!" he called, scared.

"What is this letter so early in the morning?" she asked casually.

"Doctor Bhaskar."

"What happened to him? Did he say that he was coming?" she asked leisurely.

"What is it that you are saying? He said that he is leaving this world, and that all his assets are mine!"

"What is this outrage? Go tell Ayya about it. Do you have his address?"

"Yes."

"Then let's go." She smoothed her saree and came out. Venkiah brought the car. Purna, Shekhar, Raghu, and Rambabu all went to Bhaskar's place.

Word went around that Bhaskar had passed away, and a crowd had assembled in front of the house. Lalita was devastated. His friends brought the body out to the front hall. Purnamma and Lalitamma were sitting together.

"Forgive me, Sister-in-law. I am a sinner in not realizing that the children were this madly in love. I was not able to recognize the sacredness of the love between them. I just thought that they were childish and not knowing life. They say that sins are washed away, if confessed. These children have taught me the strength of their love. I looked for money, dowry, and status. I have sacrificed the children in my ignorance. What is the use of thinking about it now? Will you forgive me please?"

Lalita fell on Purna and sobbed.

"Sister-in-law, the fault is not all yours. I have also made mistakes. Malati was very adamant that she wanted to see Bhaskar. I discouraged her. They will meet in the next world. There will not be any small-minded people like us who will hinder them there," said Purna.

Sarojini walked in with a huge rose garland and placed it on Bhaskar's body in reverence. All the rituals were performed according to tradition by Rambabu. That evening he went home, and taking the photo from his mother's box, he placed his father's picture next to the one of his mother at the nursing home. He lighted a pair of lamps in front of them and bowed down to his parents.

*~ The end ~*

# Glossary

**Amma garu, Amma**:  mother, madam
**Ayya**: father, the head of the family
**Almirah**: cupboard
**Ayah/Dayi**: maid or aide
**Ayyo/hayyo**: Oh, dear
**Bava**: male kissing cousin
**Bindi**: red dot
**Blouse piece**: widows are not given the blouse piece with a saree to denote that they are incomplete
**Chiranjeevi**: blessing for a long life
**Durvasa**: a sage known for his short temper and curses
**Emandi**: polite term in addressing another person
**Jangri/laddus**: sweets
**I'll come**: short for I will go and come (I am going/ denoting death)
**Lalchi/Jubba**: Indian shirt
**Lakhs**: hundred thousand
**Mangal Snana**: wedding bath
**Mangala sutra/Thali**: token of marriage worn around the neck
**Matrisri**: Holy mother

**Nanna**: father
**Puja**: ritual of worship
**Payas**: rice pudding
**Pan**: betel leaves wrapped with spices inside
**Pakodi/Chekodi**: kind of snacks
**Poolu**: flowers, to rhyme with Malu, short for Malati
**Rangoli**: design at the entrance of the house, using rice powder
**Sambhar**: spiced lentil
**Sister**: nurse
**Tulsi**: basil plant
**Trimurti**: the Trinity of Gods
**Upma**: dish made of semolina
**Yagna**: the rite of sacrifice

# Acknowledgements

I sincerely thank my cheerleaders and lifelong friends, Vimala Ramakrishnan and Vasantha Sundaram, who have encouraged me every step of the way. I also thank my sister, Leela, and her daughter, Malavika, for encouragement. We watched our mother wading through her handwritten manuscripts, written in the Telugu language, and never imagined that it would branch out in this manner. A special thanks to my friend from grade school Padma Hejmadi for her love and advice in all my writings. I am also indebted to my dear sons, Aditya and Soumitra, who believed in me, and last but not least, my husband, Satyasagar, for all his support.

# About the Author & Translator

## *The Author*
Kamaraju Susila 1915 – 1998
*Prema Balam* first published in 1983
(in Telugu)

Kamaraju Susila comes from a family of writers. Her father wrote about philosophy; her husband, medicine; and her brother, history. A daughter works in social sciences, a granddaughter in history, and a couple of nephews in economics and chemistry in the next generation. Susila was neither a working woman nor an academic. What could she write about? What was her specialty? She could write about LOVE.

She was married at age eleven, as her father wanted to fulfill his fatherly duties before leaving the country. In 1926, a three-month trip across the ocean to England was considered a voyage into the unknown. Preteen Susila fell madly in love with the dashing medical student who was handed over to her as a husband. This passionate love lasted throughout her lifetime and sustained her through the travails of her life. The child bride graduated from college and into a sensible, mature adult. The couple molded into each other and were sensitive to each other's needs. This love gave him strength when in despair—when he was a prisoner of war for four years in World War II in Singapore and held captive by the Japanese. That someone waited for him made him live each day with hope that the war would be over soon and that he would be back home with his family.

He preceded her in death by nine years. These years without him physically made her retreat to her childhood and her early married years. She spent the years without him living in her memories. When she died, she was enveloped in his arms with his coat that she had preserved to accompany her to the crematorium, where they were united forever.

The marriage of sixty-two years gave her the passion in love to say that the bond between a man and woman is the strongest of all relationships. It is a pity that in modern times, this has become a rarity.

## *The Translator*
### Uma Eachempati

Uma Eachempati is the daughter of the author Kamaraju Susila. She has a certificate in creative writing from Washington University, St Louis. This translation has been a labor of love. Uma lives in St Louis, Missouri, and is working on a collection of short stories. She is a retired obstetrician.

CPSIA information can be obtained
at www.ICGtesting.com
Printed in the USA
FFOW01n1749270214
3915FF

9 780991 488506